YE OLDE AN'

CW00504020

The Edw

By

Margaret Brazear

Copyright © Margaret Brazear 2018

https://www.margaret-brazear.com

TABLE OF CONTENTS

CHAPTER ONE
The Legacy

It came as no surprise to Rachel that she would inherit everything from the last of her spinster aunts. Now Aunt Iris was gone, she was the only one left in the family, an only child. She didn't think she had managed to persuade them to make a Will. She had certainly never persuaded them to do anything else, including leaving their house in later years.

The house was in a suburb of London, a very expensive suburb of London. It was a cheap area when the aunts were born there, along with their oldest brother, Charlie, and Rachel's father, David, the baby of the family.

She knew little about them. Rachel's father had died when she was a child, and his family had never approved of her mother. For that reason, there was little interaction and all Rachel knew was that the eldest brother had passed away just after the war, in the mid fifties in fact. Rachel knew nothing else about him and was never very interested.

She never found out why they had all disapproved of Rachel's mother, only that, according to her, they didn't want him to marry at all. When her mother died, she took with her any more information she might have imparted.

This morning, as Rachel left the solicitor's office after hearing the reading of a Will she had no idea her aunts had made, she felt a little mystified to learn that apart from the house, worth a few million by today's standards, there was also a shop.

"It's an unusual situation," the Solicitor said. "Your uncle was an antiques dealer and he passed away in 1955. Since then the shop has been locked up, as your aunts knew nothing about the antiques trade. It seems nobody has been inside it since then."

Rachel could only stare at him. She knew about the house, certainly, and was still undecided as to whether she should keep it and live in it, or sell it. But a shop?

The solicitor waited patiently for her reply. His name was Cyril Rhodes, a man of about sixty years with a balding head and wearing a three piece suit and a gold pocket watch, not something one saw much of nowadays. It must have been uncomfortable in this heat.

The office was one of those old fashioned places converted from buildings a few centuries old, with black beams across the ceiling and narrow, wooden stairs going up to the first and second floors. The atmosphere was oppressive, the tiny lead lighted windows letting in only a glimpse of the bright sunlight outside. The walls lined with heavy law books bound in brown and green leather added to the gloom.

Even Mr Rhodes' desk was gloomy, one of those dark wooden affairs with a green leather top. There was an electric fan in the corner, directed at his chair to cool him down, while his clients suffered.

Rachel couldn't wait to get outside. She'd worn a business suit for this meeting and she wriggled about to unstick her blouse from her perspiring skin.

"I'm sorry, Mr Rhodes," she said. "I knew nothing about a shop and I'm not sure my mother did either. You say it hasn't been opened in over sixty years? It will be full of cobwebs."

"It most certainly will."

"I don't understand why my aunts didn't sell it," Rachel went on. "They were always short of money and it appears to be in a popular and expensive area of London. It would have fetched a fair bit."

"Apparently, they felt it would be a betrayal of their late brother."

Rachel sighed impatiently. She had no time for sentimentality when it cost money.

"Ah, yes," she said. "I recall they were very sentimental, never parted with a thing. I can't say I share that particular trait."

"Well," said Mr Rhodes, "here are the keys to both the house and the shop. You can take possession any time you wish."

She gathered up the two sets of keys and stuffed them into her shoulder bag. She was in no hurry to visit the house, but the shop was another matter. No one had set foot inside in sixty years and she had no intention of going there alone.

At home in her London flat, she made herself a cup of coffee and browsed through the deeds Mr Rhodes had given her that afternoon. The shop was in a part of London she was unfamiliar with, a place where there were few retail premises and many offices. Some of those offices were converted from really old buildings, most with black and white facades on the front. The doorways were too low to get through without ducking.

Rachel knew at once who she should take with her to investigate the shop. Peter Attwood, a friend of long standing, an archaeologist and medievalist and a man who would be fascinated by a shop that had stood empty and gathering dust for over sixty years.

She drained her coffee cup and picked up the phone.

***

The city was reasonably quiet on Saturday, so quiet that Rachel was able to drive in and even park on the street. There were no red zone restrictions from Saturday afternoon through to midnight on Sunday.

From Monday to Friday, this place would be swarming with office workers and the traffic would be thick and noisy, but not at the weekends. Not many people wanted to visit this part of London at the weekends. The offices were all closed and there were no tourist attractions, unless you counted the buildings themselves.

The shop was in a side road off Holborn, nestled between black and white Tudor buildings with overhanging upper floors which looked like they might collapse at any moment.

Rachel was always fascinated by these buildings; she wondered how had they stood here, so sturdy and solid, for over five hundred years when houses constructed today would likely never last out the century. They weren't even built with proper bricks and deep foundations.

The heat wave hadn't let up. If anything it was even hotter today, but knowing English weather, it would end abruptly in a thunder storm. Rachel had dressed in the bare minimum, super short white denim shorts and a pink vest that left her midriff open to the elements.

The pair stood on the opposite side of the road and gazed at the shop. The windows were dark, although they could not tell from this distance if it was dirt that obscured the view or something else. It was nestled in between those Tudor buildings, but it wasn't Tudor. If it had been, it wouldn't have that Dickensian looking front, as these were listed buildings and the government wouldn't allow any modernisation. It seemed that this shop had been built to fill in a space.

Ye Olde Antique Shoppe, said the painted sign, actually with old fashioned spelling.

"It looks Dickensian," Peter remarked.

"It does. Looks like the Old Curiosity Shop."

"But it must be older than that, a lot older."

"Why?" Rachel said.

Peter's mouth twisted in a half smile, a patronising sort of grin.

"Look around you, Rachel, my dear, and use your noddle," he said. "How do you suppose a Victorian shop would have found its way among all this Tudor architecture? These are all listed buildings, even the upper floors of the shop are Tudor."

Rachel blushed. She hadn't noticed the upper floor when she decided this place must have been built later.

"Ok, so I wasn't thinking. Are you coming in?"

"I didn't come all this way to just stand here and admire." Peter took her arm, gave a quick glance both ways to be sure there was no approaching traffic, and hurried her across the road. "I cannot wait to get inside," he added. "If you tell me now you've forgotten to bring the keys, I'll not be responsible."

She laughed as she ran to keep up with his long strides. She wasn't as eager to get inside as he obviously was, but she was willing to give it a go. In fact, she had a sense of dread about the whole affair.

This part of London had a few quaint little shops, tobacconists that sold fancy pipes and lighters, specialist tobacco that one could buy nowhere else. She wondered how they kept going, considering not many people smoked nowadays. There were a few other specialist shops, an upper class tailor and a shop that made uniforms for the armed forces, but they were all closed on Saturday afternoons.

She could not understand why anyone would keep a shop like this antique shop standing empty, no matter how sentimental they were.

"Ready?" Peter said.

She handed him the keys, watched as he

selected the most likely one, pushed it into the keyhole and turned it.

"Is it stiff?" She asked.

"We are still talking about the lock, are we?" Peter answered with a grin.

Rachel shook her head, a gesture of despair.

"I don't know why I put up with you," she muttered. "You've got a mind like a sewer."

"Sorry, couldn't resist."

Peter used all his strength to turn the key and he thought it unlikely that Rachel would have been able to turn it on her own. Nobody had turned this key in more than sixty years; had she come alone she would have needed to bring pliers.

The door creaked so much that Rachel glanced along the road to be sure they had attracted no attention from passers by. She didn't know why that should matter, but it did. This place had the atmosphere of a haunted house, the sort one saw in films and television programmes, and her heart began to hammer as she followed Peter inside.

She had arranged with the electricity company to switch the power back on yesterday, and was relieved to see that the light switch actually lit up the overhead lamp when she clicked it.

It was a very old light switch, the sort with

the round, protruding fitting in black plastic, quite ugly compared to today's neat switches that sat flush with the wall. The cable leading down to the switch was outside the wall, secured with metal casing. It had obviously been put in after the building was erected It crossed her mind to hope the wiring was sound and safe; she half expected to see sparks.

There was a heavy wooden counter, the sort one used to see in haberdashery shops. It was dark oak with a glass front and surface and little drawers that opened at the back, where customers could see what was on offer and the shop assistant could open the drawers to get the item out for them.

Inside, she saw jewellery, costume jewellery probably. There were big old brooches, Victorian style, and heavy necklaces. There were also things like gloves, the long ones that actresses wore in those old black and white films, the sort that came up to their elbows.

There were collars too, wide lace collars that women wore over their dresses. Rachel grinned a little at the idea of wearing all this stuff. It was expected as well, not something one chose like today, where both men and women more or less wore whatever they liked and nobody even noticed.

She wondered what those staid and stately

Victorian types would think about her and Peter, dressed in a white tee shirt and faded, torn jeans as well as bare feet in open sandals.

Behind the counter were dark wooden shelves built into the wall and on them were more items from the Georgian and Victorian age, perhaps even some Regency. There were vases, picture frames with serious looking subjects staring at the camera as though it might be an instrument of execution. There were antique clocks, some with fancy carving around the face and Rachel was hoping they'd be worth a lot of money.

There was an old leather-bound photograph album on one of the bottom shelves and she picked it up and opened it, then dropped it quickly.

"What's wrong?" Peter asked.

"It's one of those books like in that film, you know the one. It's a book of the dead. Fancy taking photographs of dead people."

"You mean 'The Others'?"

She nodded.

"That's the one."

"The Victorians were very involved with the dead. They used to clip a piece of a dead person's hair and carry it about with them in lockets and bracelets. What else is there?"

Her eyes moved to the window, recalling the obscured view from outside, and it seemed it was mostly dirt that was preventing the window display from being seen. The window sill was wide enough to hold several vases, mostly Victorian Rachel thought, but she was no expert. Peter was the historian; that was why she had brought him.

"It's good, isn't it?" he remarked now.

"Is it?"

"Oh, come on girl. You can't deny this is fascinating."

"Can't I? I'll be more interested when I find out how much this stuff's worth." She picked up a vase that seemed to be porcelain with a flower pattern apparently hand painted all round it. "What about this?"

"Georgian, I think," he said. "Can't be sure though. We'll need to get an antique dealer in to value it and this other stuff. The gloves are probably from the twenties or thirties, not that old. But then there are some that go higher up the arm; they might be older. I don't know a lot about ladies' fashion."

"Really? I thought it would be right up your street."

"Don't get sarky or I'll go home."

She shook her head, reached for his arm and rested her head against it.

"I don't think you'll abandon all this. Anyway, what's in there?"

She had only just noticed the door into the back of the shop. It was panelled and dark wood, blended in with the rest of the woodwork. She found another one of those ugly light switches beside this new door and clicked it on. The light showed up the door with its brass doorknob and something else neither of them had noticed before. Attached to the door with brass screws was a plaque, also in brass, and the engraving was clear, if slightly diminished by sixty years of grime.

The contents of this room must never be removed from these premises.

Their eyes met, hers wide and full of wonder, his creased from a frown. He smiled mischievously.

"Shall we look first, or wait here and try to guess why the contents of this room must never be removed from these premises?" said Peter.

He seemed to think it was some sort of game, but Rachel felt a shiver and goosepimples erupted on her bare arms.

"I don't think it's funny, Pete," she said. "There's a reason no one tried to sell this place, a reason no one has been here for sixty years."

"Yes, there is, and I for one can't wait to find out what that reason is. You can't tell me you're not intrigued."

"Yes, I am," she replied. "But I also find it scary."

"Scary? Why?"

"More to the point, why don't you?"

He put his arm around her and hugged her, kissed her forehead then took a step to guide her toward the mysterious door.

"Perhaps because life isn't as serious as you think it is," he replied. "Now, can we please have a look? Or have we come all this way for nothing?"

"All right," she agreed reluctantly. "I suppose we'll have to. But behave, please. I've got a feeling this is serious stuff, whether you like it or not."

He released her, stood to attention and saluted, clicking his heels together as he did so.

"Whatever you say, Ma'am," he replied.

She was still nervous about opening that door, but it seemed unlikely she would ever convince Peter that she had good reason for it. She nodded, watched with mounting dread as he found the right key on the set he still held in his hand.

The door opened slowly, but surprisingly smoothly. It was a heavy door and Peter had to push it with his shoulder to get it to open fully. Rachel stared at it hesitantly, then looked about for something with which to prop it open. She found a stool, a dark wooden affair with steps that pulled out from under the seat, obviously used for reaching the higher shelves behind the counter.

She settled it in the open doorway, much to Peter's amusement.

"What are you doing that for?" He asked.

"Just in case."

"In case what? In case the ghoulies and ghosties come along and shut us in?"

He gestured with his hands and fingers as he spoke, making ghost noises like a kid at Halloween.

"Grow up, Pete, please," she said. "You might find it funny, but I'm scared. Whoever had that plaque made and went to the trouble of screwing it into the door, did so for a reason."

"Of course he did," Peter replied. "Because he was batty, that's why."

"Or because he thought it was important. Anyway, it's only sensible. Supposing we do get shut inside; nobody knows we're here."

Peter shoved his hand in the pocket of his faded jeans and pulled out a smartphone. He held it up, wiggling his hand about theatrically.

"I know," she insisted. "I know, I know, but I've got a strong feeling that won't work in there."

Now his laughter rang out as he pushed his

phone back in his pocket and took her hand.

"Come on, you silly mare," he said. "Or do you want to stay out here so you can rescue me if I get stuck?"

As he pushed the door open fully, Rachel reached up and found the light switch. It was outside this room, a bit like they sometimes have in bathrooms, which she thought was odd. Perhaps this had once been such a closet of some sort; there was no window in here, no natural light at all.

She almost collided with Peter as he stopped suddenly and she wondered if he'd seen something which frightened him too. Serve him right if he had, after taking the piss out of her worries.

But then she saw what had caused him to stop in his tracks and look around in wonder.

"My God," he muttered and she noticed that he sort of breathed the word, rather than spoke it.

"What is it?"

She released her hand from his and moved past him to look around the room. There were round wooden poles sticking out from the walls, each one containing clothes, but not modern clothes. Some of them were Elizabethan, with the heavy brocade and the wide skirts. There were Tudor doublets for men as well and other things she didn't recognise.

She stepped forward, reached out and pulled a waistcoat toward her. On the same hanger was some of those awful men's knickers she had seen in portraits and television plays. She held them up, two separate legs of bright scarlet and gold satin.

"How could any woman fancy a man wearing bloomers?" she asked. "I'm surprised this fashion didn't bring an end to the human race."

"It might well have done, had women had any choice in the matter."

"What do you mean?"

He shook his head slowly, mockingly.

"I knew you didn't know a lot about history, but I thought everyone knew how women were treated in the past."

"How? How were they treated?"

"They were property, nothing more. They were married off to men they'd never laid eyes on and had no say in their own lives at all." He paused and his eyes met hers. "You wouldn't last five minutes."

"I wouldn't want to."

She still held the hanger with the Tudor bloomers hanging from it and attached to them was a thing that looked like a single bra cup and had a long tie fastening.

She turned to Peter, holding it out.

"What on earth is this for?" she asked.

He touched the object, felt the solid shell of the thing, and smiled hesitantly.

"You've seen those pictures of Henry VIII haven't you? It's the thing he wore at the front of himself, to protect his dangly bits, and to show off. It's a codpiece."

Rachel blushed a little and grimaced.

"It's disgusting," she said. "But look at all these clothes. I wonder what they're doing here."

"I think they are part of the stock, the ones we must in no circumstances remove from this shop."

"Do you mean you think they're genuine?" Rachel gripped the skirt of a gown and held it up. "This looks like something I've seen in portraits of Elizabeth I. I seem to recall that the oldest thing they have in the Victoria and Albert is the remains of a petticoat of some sort. Nothing this old survives and if it did, that's where it would be, in a museum."

"There are older things than this. They've found five thousand year old shirts and even trousers that are thousands of years old. I think these are genuine." He picked up the skirt of a gown that hung on a strong pole. He supposed a modern coat hanger would be too fragile to hold the weight of such a garment. "I could be wrong," he went on, turning it to show her the inside of the seam, "but look at the stitching, and the thread. Definitely hand stitched and the thread's really thick."

Peter stared at the clothes for a few more minutes before he turned his attention to the dark oak shelves and drawers in the corner. The top one had jewels, all of which looked genuine to him, but the second drawer down contained coins.

"This is all fascinating stuff," Rachel remarked. "I suppose he put that plaque on the door to scare away thieves or something."

Peter was shaking his head, slowly, thoughtfully. He stood in front of the cabinet and stared at the coins in the open drawer.

"What have you found that's struck you dumb?" Rachel asked.

She crossed the room and stood beside him, took his arm and peered past him to the cabinet. The coins looked old but not as old as the Roman ones she'd seen in museums; she couldn't decide what had caught Peter's attention so intensely.

He was the historian; he was the one who knew about this stuff, not her. If truth be told, she had always found history to be a boring subject and when her friend started on his historical facts, she had to suppress a yawn. But she couldn't deny that finding all this old stuff in here was piquing her interest.

Peter took a coin from the drawer and held it close to his eyes. It was fairly light in this room, light enough to see the detail, and his intense interest gave her a little thrill. She knew he was the right person to bring on this trip.

"Well?" she said.

He held out the coin to her for just a second, before he brought it back close to his own eyes to scrutinise it some more.

"It might be a fake," he said. "But I don't think it is. Why would anyone put that plaque on the door if there was anything fake in here?"

"Well, come on, Pete," she said with exasperation. "What is it?"

"It's a gold coin with the Archangel Michael and the name of Edward V."

He glanced at her briefly, somehow expecting her to know what that meant, but of course she didn't.

"Which one was he?"

"You've heard about the princes in the Tower, haven't you?" He answered. "Even you must know that story."

She nodded.

"Yes, but they were princes, not kings."

"One of them was. Edward was King Edward V, albeit briefly, and his uncle, who later became

Richard III, had coins minted in his name in preparation for the coronation."

"I didn't know there was a coronation."

Peter smiled indulgently.

"There wasn't, but Richard prepared for one just the same. Many people believe it was all part of the facade, to make people think he was protecting the princes and would crown young Edward as King. It never happened and the princes disappeared, but for any of those coins to have survived is something of a miracle."

"Worth a bit, then?" Rachel remarked.

She was gradually realising how much money she could get for all this stuff, even without selling the freehold to the shop and the house. In fact, it might be enough to let her keep the house and live in it.

"If it's genuine, Rachel, old girl," said Peter, "it's worth a small fortune, maybe even a big one."

He pulled his smartphone out of his pocket with the intention of typing in a search for the coin, but the phone was dead, completely dead. The screen was completely blank as though it had been turned off. He said nothing to Rachel; she already had the heebie jeebies about this room, so he shoved the phone back into his pocket.

"So we'll take it home," said Rachel, "get on

the internet and look up coin dealers. Are there any more in there?"

"Lots, but this is the only Edward V. They'll all be worth a fair bit, I should think, but none as much as this one."

CHAPTER TWO
The World Outside

Rachel wanted to spend more time in that room, going through the rest of the stuff with Peter, but he was anxious to get home, to look for coin dealers and discover just how rare and valuable the coin was.

"You stay," he said. "I'll get the underground home."

Rachel shook her head.

"No, Pete," she said. "I don't want to stay here alone. It's creepy."

Again he laughed. He was enjoying her discomfort, there was no doubt about that, because he could not understand it.

"These things are beautiful, Rachel," he said. "How can you call them creepy? We'll come back later or tomorrow, see what else is there. But I'd like to find a dealer today; tomorrow's Sunday and I don't think my nerves will wait till Monday."

"Ok," she answered gloomily. "But I'm not staying here by myself. I'm coming with you."

Again, he grinned, but his stomach fluttered with excitement as he put the coin in his pocket, followed her out of the little room and locked the door.

"This coin must be so rare, Rachel," he said. "Do you realise how few of these were minted?"

In the outer room, the main sales floor, he once again pulled out his smartphone. Now it worked, didn't even need switching on. He could see no reason why anything should be different here than in the back room. Perhaps it was the lack of windows. Rachel waited while he connected to a website to look up the coin. His eyes grew wide.

"Well?" she said. "You've obviously found something."

"The last one of these found was in a field in Dorset. It sold for nearly £50,000."

"Wow," she said. "Can you just imagine how much the rest of this stuff will sell for? There could be more coins in there, more that are worth as much. Then there's all the clothes and the jewels." She paused and sighed. "Oh, Pete, this is incredible. Why on earth did my uncle not sell all this stuff? I wonder if my aunts even knew what was in here. They lived from hand to mouth on their pensions."

"Who knows?" Pete felt that the coin was still in the pocket of his jeans. "Let's go. My heart's going so fast, I think you might have to drive me to the nearest casualty department if we don't get on with it."

She didn't tell him that she felt the same,

though probably for different reasons. Peter had degrees in archaeology and in medieval history and worked at the London Museum, cataloguing antiquities, so this stuff was all very exciting to him. Rachel, on the other hand, was interested in the amount of money she could get and she wanted to get rid of this place as soon as it could be arranged.

She had been designing women's clothes for one of the top London designers since she left university two years ago and her ambition was to start her own design house, her own label. The money from the antiquities in this shop could be just enough to start her off.

She couldn't sell the shop as a going concern, since it hadn't been a working business for more than sixty years, but she could put all this stuff up for auction at one of the big auction houses. She was thinking about the credit card bills she couldn't afford to pay and the lovely new car she would really like to buy. And if she could afford to live in the aunts' house, she wouldn't have to pay rent and she would be very well off.

She'd have to give Pete something for his help; she might even rent him a couple of rooms in the house. He wasn't happy with the place he was in now and they got on very well together.

Rachel opened the front door and stepped outside. The heat seemed to have cooled somewhat while they had been inside as that was the first thing she noticed, and she would be thankful for the jacket she kept in the car.

Peter followed with the keys clutched tightly in his hand, then he turned and locked the door while she waited, gazing across a dirt track at the tethered horses grazing in the fields on the other side, at the ancient wooden coach that passed in front of them, drawn by two horses.

"Give us a bit of room, girl," Peter said as he pushed at her back to gain more space.

She took one step away from him, felt the uneven surface beneath her feet, then she turned back and clutched at his tee shirt, almost ripping the fabric.

"Pete," she whispered hoarsely.

"Come on, Rachel, give us a break. You're choking me." Leaving the key hanging from the lock, he turned to look at her. "What's wrong?"

His eyes moved passed her and he gasped.

"It's real, isn't it?" she muttered. "I'm not imagining it, am I?"

He pulled her into his arms, clutched her so tightly she thought her bones might break, but she clung to him just the same. She didn't want to turn round, didn't want to look again. She moved her head to look along the row of buildings in which the antique shop was nestled; they had been Tudor buildings, black and white, with overhanging upper floors.

Now all she saw was slatted wooden walls. It was a long barn, with no windows and a thatched roof.

The next thing she noticed was the quiet.

"Peter, there's no traffic, nothing."

He swallowed hard. He tried to be brave, tried to comfort her, but he could not deny he was just as frightened as she was. He looked along the dirt track, saw a horse pulling a rickety wooden carriage of some sort. Then the coach drew to a stop and two women alighted. His eyes moved to stare at those fields again and that's when they heard the scream.

Rachel turned toward the sound and her eyes fixed on the figures on the other side of the dirt track, the women who had got down from that coach. There were two of them, one dressed in fine velvet that gathered on the ground around her feet with a short train fashioned into the skirt. The other wore a white bonnet of some sort and a pale grey dress of some lightweight fabric with a smocked bodice of the type babies used to wear.

Now they stared at Peter and Rachel as though they had seen a ghost and perhaps they had.

The poorer dressed of the two women crossed herself, closed her eyes briefly and muttered something. The dirt track was not very wide and the couple could easily hear the startled words of the lady in velvet.

"Harlot," she gasped, then clutched the hand of what was probably her servant. "Whore!"

Peter looked down at Rachel's shorts, her summer sandals, her sleeveless top, looked at his own torn and faded denim jeans and tee shirt and he knew precisely what had troubled these two women.

He turned quickly and reached for the keys that still hung from the lock. He fumbled with them, his hands shaking as he desperately tried to get inside before anyone else saw them. Rachel still stood rigidly and stared across the track at the sumptuously dressed woman on the other side.

Her hair was curled on top of her head beneath a headdress of the sort she had seen in portraits in some of those stately homes Peter had persuaded her to visit. Her bodice was so tight it caused her bosom to wobble above her neckline and Rachel noticed that neckline was stitched with pearls.

That was all she saw before Peter gripped her arm and pulled her inside the shop. She stumbled as he slammed the door behind them and reached out to catch her. Both were breathing rapidly, so fast they thought their hearts would break out of their chests.

Rachel slid down the wall to land on the floor of the shop and Peter followed suit. They clutched each other's hands so tightly Peter felt her fingernails digging into his palm.

"What was that?" Rachel said at last.

Her eyes were moving rapidly around their surroundings, just to be sure it was the same shop they had entered that morning, naively excited by the prospect of exploring a shop that had not been opened for more than sixty years.

"I can't believe I'm saying this," Peter replied, "but I think we just proved there is such a thing as a time slip."

"What? What the Hell's a time slip?"

"I've read about people who have had glimpses of the past, just a few seconds, not even enough to be sure really."

"That's what this was?" Rachel said. "And these people; did they ever repeat the experience? Or could they go back to the same place and find everything as it should be?"

Peter shrugged.

"I don't know. I always thought they were nuts, or imagining things or more likely making it up to get attention. I didn't take too much notice."

"Well, genius, it would seem you were wrong. Did you hear what that woman called me?"

"A harlot."

"Yes, a harlot. Not a word you'd hear much today." She frowned thoughtfully and leaned closer to Peter. "These reports of time slips," she said. "Did they mention anyone talking?"

He shook his head.

"Not that I know of. If these tales are right," he said, "when we go outside again, everything should be back to normal."

"Why did she call me that?" Rachel asked. "I mean, why would anyone say that to someone they've never seen before?"

He put his arms around her and gave her a hug.

"It was the way you're dressed," he said. "Shorts up to your bum and your arms and middle showing."

"Oh. I understand the legs, but the arms?"

"If you look at any medieval portraits you'll see that none of the ladies have their arms showing. Apparently it was ok to show most of your boobs, but not your arms."

She pushed herself up till she was standing. Her knees were still a bit wobbly from the shock, but she managed to feel her way along the counter to the front window. Leaning over the wide shelf that held the window display, she rubbed at the grime until she had made a patch she could see through. She breathed a sigh of relief to see the familiar sight of the narrow London street with a few Saturday afternoon cars travelling slowly along. There was even a bus, a beautiful big, red London bus, a sight she would never have believed would ever be so welcome.

"It's ok, Pete," she said. "Everything's back where it's supposed to be. We can go home now and not tell anyone about this. They'll think we're crazy."

She turned to Peter, who still sat on the hard floor, holding the Angel Edward V coin, studying it closely.

"The plaque on the door," he said.

"What about it?"

"It said not to remove anything from this shop, anything that was inside that room."

"Yes, so what?"

She bent and took his hand, pulled him to his feet, then he went back to the room where they had found the coin. He opened the door and stepped inside.

"Look around you, Rachel," Peter said. "No one has been in here for sixty years, but in this room there is no dust, no cobwebs. In the main shop it looks like it's been abandoned, but not here. Even the air smells fresh."

"What? You think someone's been coming

here and cleaning just this room?"

"No, that's not what I think at all."

"What then?" she said. "Stop talking in riddles."

"Don't you see? The buildings along this row, except for this shop are Tudor. At some point the front of this one has been updated, but not the rest. When we went outside before, these buildings were all gone."

"Yes, a time slip," she answered. "You said before."

"But suppose it was more than that. Supposing it was this coin."

"The coin?" she repeated.

"Yes," he said thoughtfully. "Out there was pre-Tudor, perhaps even Plantagenet, around the time of King Edward V. This part was just a village then, not even that and certainly not part of London. Perhaps that's why we're not supposed to take anything out of here, because if we do, we'll be taking it back to its own time."

She laughed. She'd got over the sheer terror of finding herself in another time, accepted Peter's explanation that it was just a fluke, and now she thought his suggestion was bizarre.

"You're daft," she said. "That coin is worth a fortune and if you're right, which would be ridiculous, I can't sell it."

"Not only that," he answered. "You can't sell

anything in here, nothing at all."

She sighed impatiently, then went to the front door and opened it. Outside was quiet for London, but no more than one would expect for a Saturday afternoon in the city.

"Look," she said, stepping outside. "Everything's where it should be. There's my car; it hasn't turned into a horse and carriage, or a pumpkin."

He followed her outside, looked gingerly up and down the road and into High Holborn and bit his lip.

"Where's the coin?" Rachel asked.

"I left it inside."

"Oh, for God's sake," she said, then she turned and marched back into the shop. There on the counter was the glittering coin with the Archangel Michael engraved on its surface, its uneven edges showing it to be ancient. Her heart fluttered a little; she couldn't wait to get this coin to the auction house.

She picked it up, her mind full of the BMW she'd had her eye on, and she stepped outside to join her friend. But he was gone and that dirt track was back, along with the fields and the wooden buildings with the thatched roofs.

"Peter!" She shouted, her heart hammering.

There was no reply, none at all, but across that dirt track stood a young boy, about sixteen and he was staring at her with wide eyed disapproval. She looked down at her clothes, then fled back inside the shop. She threw the coin at the corner of the room and turned back to the front door, her relief at seeing Peter standing in the doorway so overwhelming, she almost fainted.

"Are you coming or what?" He said.

She flung herself into his arms, like some feeble female from that past she had just visited. She had to remind herself that she was a successful career woman of the twenty first century, not some uneducated and helpless girl, needing a man's comfort and protection.

"Oh, Pete," she mumbled against his shirt. "You were right."

"I was?"

"Did you see what happened? Did you see where I went?"

He shook his head.

"I was just waiting for you to come back out."

"I did, and I took the coin. I was back there again, with the barns and the dirt track and the fields. And you were nowhere to be seen. I was bloody terrified."

"I don't blame you," he answered. "Where's the coin?"

She shrugged.

"In there somewhere. I threw it. I suppose

we'd better go and put it back where it belongs, in that strange room. Otherwise someone might steal it."

Peter laughed cynically.

"They'd get a shock if they did, wouldn't they?" He pushed her gently away. "I think the best thing we can do is go back to your place and discuss things, decide what to do next."

CHAPTER THREE
The First Foray

The coffee was strong and flavourful and Rachel stood staring out of her first floor window at the traffic while she sipped it. She'd added lots of cream, real cream not milk, as she wanted to taste something twenty first century to anchor her to the present time. She had an idea that cream was modern, but she wasn't sure. Coffee most certainly was, or at least she thought it was. Pete would know, but she didn't want to ask.

He lounged on the sofa, sipping his own sweet drink. Five spoonfuls of sugar in his coffee was the norm, but Rachel didn't believe he was as nonchalant about their morning's adventure as he pretended.

"Is it for the shock?" She asked him.

"What?"

"All that sugar. Is it for the shock?"

"Partly. You know I always have a lot of sugar in coffee, but I admit it. I'm feeling a bit shaky still."

She glanced back at him, but only for a second before she fixed her eyes firmly on the road once more.

"You're not alone," she said.

"Come and sit down," Peter said. "We need to talk about this. Aren't you just dying to talk about it? I am."

"Yes. Yes, I want to talk about it, but I also need to be sure the traffic is still there."

"What?"

He put his coffee cup on the side table and pushed himself up, cross the room to stand behind her.

"I'm finding it soothing," she said. "The cars, the buses, the traffic lights, even the horns from impatient drivers. That's us, Pete. That's our time out there and the more I look at it, the more I distrust my memory."

"Come and sit down," he said again. "Let's go over it. Come and look at this."

She followed him to the sofa, where he had set his laptop on the coffee table and found a website that talked about reported time slips.

"Well," she said. "You can find any old rubbish on the internet. I saw a website the other week 'proving' that the earth's flat. Well, it must be right, because it's on the internet."

"But look at all the reported time slips there have been, Rache."

"But it wasn't a time slip, was it?" She said. "If it was, it wouldn't have happened again when I tried to take the coin out of the shop and you stayed behind, in our time. And now I know why nobody every tried to sell the place. My aunts must have known."

"Perhaps they did."

"Then why the hell didn't they tell me?" Rachel fought to control her rising voice. "Why did they let me discover this for myself?"

"Would you have believed them if they had?"

She stared at him, her mind busy, and knew he was right. No, she would not have believed them. She'd have thought they'd gone senile.

"All right, I wouldn't have believed them. But this means I can't sell the shop either and I can't sell any of the stuff inside it."

"There're the things in the front shop, in the window. Those vases looked valuable."

"Hardly the same thing. I'll just have to write it off, won't I? It won't be worth anything now. I can't sell it; I don't want to run it and there's not enough valuable stock that I can sell to make it worth while." She sipped more of her coffee, sighed impatiently. She felt like crying, but thought that a bit silly. "It's worthless."

"Oh, I wouldn't say that," Peter said. "I can think of many uses for it."

"What?"

"Well, you're a designer. You could set up shop in the front; there's plenty of room for your workshop and you might even get some ideas from those clothes in the back."

He was right. It could well be used as a shop front for her own design house, if the place ever stopped giving her the shivers.

"I'm not sure I could work in there," she said. "I'd be scared of ghosts."

"Or..." He began, then hesitated for a moment.

"Or?"

"We could organise tours to the past. We'd make a fortune."

She coughed up her drink, put the cup down on the coffee table and shook her head at him. Still, she wasn't sure he was joking.

"I do believe you're serious."

"Why not? Just think what it would mean to historians."

"And when they go and murder our ancestors or warn Anne Boleyn against marrying the King? We'd lose out on Elizabeth I and we'd probably all be Catholic."

He laughed mischievously. It hadn't been a serious thought; after all, he knew better than to suggest such a thing, but his suggestion had achieved its goal which was to cheer her up, get her mind off their weird experience.

He drained his cup, studied her thoughtfully for a few minutes before he spoke again.

"I want to go back," he said at last.

"What? You must be off your trolley."

"Think of the possibilities, Rachel," he argued.

"I have. I've thought about being burned at the stake as a witch; I've thought about whatever else they did to harlots. I've already been called that."

"We didn't burn witches in this country," Peter replied. "We hanged them. After they survived the ducking stool and being poked with pins to find the Devil's mark, the bit that didn't hurt."

"Oh, that's all right then," she said sarcastically.

"They burned heretics though, so you'd better keep your atheist ideas to yourself."

She shook her head.

"I won't have to. I'm not going."

"Oh come on, Rache! We could go there with the coin; we might even discover what really happened to the princes in the Tower. If we could bring back proof, we might be able to write a book and get a bestseller."

"We can't bring anything back," she said. "If we take it out of the shop, it'll just take us back to where it came from."

"We don't know that. It might just be the stuff in that room that can't leave the shop. Don't you want to find out?"

"No."

"Rachel, please. I can't go on my own."

"Well, take one of your boyfriends with you then."

"I don't think that'd be a good idea. Being gay carried the death penalty. And it wasn't very humane, either."

She laughed, though why she could not have said.

"Will you be hung, drawn and quartered?" She said mockingly.

"No, burnt alive. And it's 'hanged' not hung. Curtains are hung; people are hanged."

"They were obviously barbarians," she said. "Why the hell you'd want to go there, I can't imagine, but I'm not going with you."

"We'll talk about it later. I fancy a takeaway; have you got a menu?"

"In the kitchen," she replied. "There's Indian and Chinese as well as the pizza place. Chinese'll do me. Are you paying?"

His mouth twisted thoughtfully as he looked at her. He doubted he'd persuade her back into the past for the price of a Chinese meal, but he hadn't given up yet. He found the menu and picked up the phone; he knew what she'd want, the same as she always had.

"Supposing it wasn't a time slip," she said while they waited for their meal to be delivered.

"What else?"

"Perhaps it was ghosts."

"Ghosts? You believe in ghosts but not in time slips?"

"Well, let's face it, they make more sense. I can more believe that the surviving spirit of a dead person is knocking about than that we can slip back in time."

"Well, yes, but what about the rest of it?" He paused, considering her suggestion then dismissing it. "The fields, the old wooden carriage, the barns where those gorgeous Tudor buildings had been. They couldn't all be ghosts. Phantoms appear in a contemporary setting; they don't bring their background with them."

The doorbell rang and Peter got up to take delivery of his Chinese dinner. He was very hungry, but refrained from thinking of himself as 'starving' when he considered where he had been that afternoon.

Following this thought was a memory of a television play he'd once seen, about some rich yuppy types who bought an old cottage and spent Christmas there with friends. They found they couldn't eat or drink anything and they kept seeing a woman and her children who had starved to death there.

He shivered. He wouldn't mention that to Rachel, or she'd never agree to go with him. At the moment, he had the advantage in that she knew little about history.

They dished out their meals on plates and sat at the small kitchen table to eat in silence for a few minutes. For Rachel's part, she was still thinking about his suggestion that she use the shop as a workshop for her designs. She'd always wanted her own design label, her own fashion house.

"I won't open it to the public," she said, as though he knew what she'd been thinking. "But you're right. Those clothes could give me some ideas and if I move the counter out of the way, I'll have plenty of room for a few cutting tables and sewing machines."

He smiled silently.

"It's a good idea," he said. "You might get a few bob for that counter." He reached out and took her hand, squeezed it tightly and gave her that playful grin that she could never resist. "Oh, please, Rachel. Let's go and have another look. We can wear some of those clothes and we won't look any different to anyone else."

His enthusiasm must have been contagious, as she felt a little flutter of excitement of her own, along with a dart of fear.

"All right," she said. "But only for a little while. I'm not staying there long enough for anything awful to happen."

He put his knife and fork down and reached

across the table to hug her tightly, his mind full of how he would get from Holborn to the Tower in 1483 so he could find evidence of what had happened to the princes.

***

"How will we know which clothes are right for the period?" Rachel asked as she moved the elaborate gowns along their poles. "Come to think of it, what'll happen if we go outside with more than one thing in our pocket, from different times?"

"It's something to think about," Peter replied. "Let's take our time though. We don't want to test it out yet."

What he was thinking about was not her question, but that nothing was going to stand in the way of him seeing the princes.

"I can't reach these," she said.

"Well, that's what that little step ladder thing's for."

"I'm not taking that out of the doorway."

He sighed impatiently and left what he was doing, sorting through the clothes to find something he could wear. He stepped over to the poles of female clothes and reached passed her to bring down an elaborate gown which was covered in tiny pearls.

A memory flashed through his mind of something he had read about clothing and different classes not being allowed to wear various fabrics, but he took little notice. He was too excited and far too eager to get outside and make his way to the Tower.

"Look," he said. "There's a number sewn into the back of this. Looks like a date."

He moved along the rows of gowns and found that each one was arranged in date order.

"Oh, well that solves that problem," said Rachel.

"Your uncle must have done this to make sure you never went through the door with two different eras on you. So, this one he must have brought back from 1482, which should be ok for our purposes."

He held up a lovely satin dress with a surcoat of heavy brocade, trimmed with fur. She fingered the trimming and shook her head.

"I can't wear that," she said. "It's real fur and it weighs a ton. I shan't be able to walk in it." She reached passed him to a grey linen dress which was simply made and not nearly so elaborate or heavy. "What about this one?"

He shrugged.

"Why not? It'll be easier to wear, that's for certain."

He took down the costume he'd been looking

at before she interrupted and searched for a date. 1481; that would do. He started to pull off his jeans while Rachel changed into her own medieval attire. She was beginning to be just as excited about this as he was and could only hope nothing terrible happened. With a bit of luck, the slip wouldn't happen again, they'd stay in twenty first century London with the traffic and the pollution and she'd be able to sell the Angel coin after all.

"Well, how do I look?" Peter asked.

He was wearing a thigh length jacket, quilted in velvet with gold thread running through it and sort of hose, but not like ladies' tights. These were a much heavier material, but they clung to his legs. They weren't half bad legs either, Rachel thought. Pity he wasn't into women.

The boots were suede, soft suede and coming to the ankles and he had found a hat in the same dark blue velvet as the jacket.

"Very handsome," she answered. "What about me?"

"I think you'd better wear some sort of hat," he said. "Your hair's too short; it might cause a problem."

"Well, surely I can wear my hair however I like, can't I? Who's going to stop me?"

"Well, old love," he said, "the last thing you want to do is cause gossip. Women wore their hair down to their waists with a head covering. I think it might be safest."

She found a white linen bonnet and put it on, tying it under her chin.

"This do?" She asked.

"I hope so."

He opened the drawer that contained the Angel coin and took it out, put it into the little drawstring purse that was tied to his fancy jacket and took Rachel's hand, squeezed it for a second before he opened the front door and stepped outside.

There was the dirt track, the fields with tethered, grazing horses, no traffic at all. He turned and locked the door of what was now a barn and stepped back, releasing Rachel's hand as he did so. The door had changed, but not the lock. That was still the same and he wondered briefly if it was authentic for the time.

His eyes moved along the row of windowless barns and his heart began to beat faster. This was an historian's dream, but oh, so scary.

They walked to the end of the street, then turned to look along toward the city, or rather where the city was on the map he'd looked up last night.

"I wonder if they have some sort of cabs for hire," he muttered, more to himself than to her.

"And what are you going to pay for it with? If

you spend that coin, we might not be able to get home."

"That's something we haven't thought about," he said. "No, I won't be spending this. Looks like it's going to be a long walk."

"A long walk where?"

"To the Tower."

She stepped back, shaking her head again.

"We'll end up in the bleedin' Tower if you're not careful."

"I want to see the princes," he admitted. "Didn't you guess?"

She sighed resignedly.

"Ok, let's go."

"Really?"

"Why not? We'll probably never make it back in one piece anyway, so we might as well make the most of it."

He took her hand and they started to walk, the dust from the road floating up and settling on their clothes. It was so quiet here it was almost impossible to imagine what it would be like in six hundred years. There were a few people in the distance, too far away to see clearly, but they seemed to be leading huge horses, the sort one saw pulling coaches and carts. They reminded Peter of the rag and bone man's horse in that tv programme, Steptoe and Son.

As they got further along the road, the area seemed to be a bit more populated, but what they noticed more than anything was the way people stared at them.

"I don't suppose they see many strangers," Rachel remarked.

The sound of hooves approaching from behind made them turn sharply, then quickly step to the side of the road before the horses ran them over. The riders didn't seem to be taking any precautions against it, at any rate.

There were two horsemen and they drew rein and stopped a few feet passed Rachel and Peter. They were very elaborately dressed, suits similar to that which Peter wore but in sumptuous satin and both were heavily adorned with jewellery. The gloves they wore showed the outline of various rings and there were heavy chains around their necks, with what looked like precious stones embedded in them. They also wore enormous brooches with rubies and diamonds forming some sort of unrecognisable pattern.

Talk about over the top!

Their saddles looked too heavy for the horses and were awkward with high backs which Rachel was sure had a name, but she wasn't sure what it was. The saddles were also chased with silver and she supposed all this flashiness made them appear important in this era. Rachel just thought they looked like a couple of first class pratts.

"Sir," one of these men called out in an imperious voice. "You disgrace your fellow man by walking so, beside your whore in public."

"Damn cheek!" Rachel cried, and would have said more had Peter not squeezed her hand, almost breaking the bones to stop her.

Both riders glared at her.

"You deserve a flogging for speaking thus to your betters," the first one said.

"You should not elevate your servant like this," his companion said.

Peter gripped her hand tighter before she had a chance to reply.

"I had thought in this quiet part, no one would notice, Sir," Peter said. He bowed awkwardly. "Forgive me if I have caused offence."

"Very well, but keep your whore behind you in public."

"Your name, Sir?" The second man demanded.

Peter had to think quickly. He'd obviously not given enough thought to this period before he stepped into it and now he had to rescue them both.

"Given the circumstances, Sir," he replied,

"I'd rather not disclose it."

Both men sniggered before riding away while Peter sighed with relief.

"What the hell was that?" Rachel demanded.

"Something I should have thought about. You must walk behind me for the rest of the journey."

"Not likely," she said. "We're going back so I can dress as fancy as you."

CHAPTER FOUR
The Princes in the Tower

Back at the shop, Peter sat on the Chesterfield in the front and booted up his laptop. It didn't seem to work in the antiques room, where all the real value was, only here.

"What are you doing?" Rachel asked.

"I'm looking up some names, just to be sure they didn't really exist. We need an identity."

"Why?"

"One thing I forgot."

"Only one thing," she said sarcastically. "That bloke wasn't joking you know."

He looked up at her thoughtfully. He could see she was shaken and he didn't blame her, but neither did he want her to decide she wasn't going again.

"I forgot that different classes wore different fabrics and colours, by law. You were dressed as a servant and I was dressed as an aristocrat, yet we were walking down the road holding hands."

"Well, what are we going to do about it? I don't want to be threatened by some pompous pratt again."

"We need identities. We'll have to pretend to be married, it's the only way."

"What about Lord and Lady Wentworth?"

His fingers moved quickly over the keyboard.

"He's on Wikipedia," Peter said. "He was a baron, so no, we can't use him."

"Smith?" She suggested cynically.

"Attwood," he said. "I can't find a Lord Attwood, so that's who we'll be. Then there's the language. I think we'd better be a baron and baroness from up north somewhere. That way they might not think it odd that they haven't heard of us and it's a good excuse for the funny accent. We'll say as little as possible, pretend we don't understand them very well." He looked up at her hopefully. "How does that sound?"

"As long as I don't have to walk behind you."

"No, but you'll have to hold my arm. Women were subservient to their menfolk, at least in public. Do you think you can manage that?"

"No, but if it keeps me alive and unmaimed I might."

"Good. Let's find you some clothes."

Rachel went into the front of the shop and opened one of the drawers behind the counter. She had seen something there yesterday that might come in handy today, and she took out the gold wedding ring and slipped it onto her finger.

She went back to Peter, waving her left hand about.

"If we're going to be married," she said. "I thought this'd do."

"It might," he answered. "But it needs to be on your right hand. They didn't wear their wedding bands on their left hand until later on."

"Oh. I thought it had something to do with being the side of the heart."

"You might well be right," he said. "But not until later. I'm not sure they even knew which side the heart was until later."

She changed the ring to her right hand then watched as he rummaged through the poles of clothes, looking for the right ones.

"I think your uncle made a point of collecting clothes for middle nobility," Peter said. "There seem to be a lot of those and only a couple of servants' garments. I've looked up the period and this is what they wore. There's nothing too fancy here, no purple or cloth of gold. That was just for royalty and no ermine, either."

"Thank God for that."

"You don't believe in God."

"That's how come I can use his name in vain." She turned to face him and held out her skirts. "Now, how do I look?"

"Magnificent," he said and she did.

The dress he'd found for her was a pale blue silk with a tight bodice under the main garment, and a waistline set just a little above the natural waist. The sleeves were laced at the cuff and she wore a hat, a headdress that was set back on her head with a flimsy veil hanging from it. The hem was bound and gathered about her feet so she'd have to hold it up to move.

"I thought people back then were shorter than us," she said. "I'm five foot four and this thing is still too long."

"I read somewhere that they did it so they had to sort of slide their feet along, making them look like they were gliding. It was to set them apart from the lower classes."

"How ridiculous," she scoffed, but she had to admit she couldn't resist twirling around in front of the mirror.

She found some loops sewn into the skirt that she could push her fingers through to hold it up but she thought the train at the back would get on her nerves.

Peter was still wearing his original costume and looked very handsome in his velvet hat and the beautiful velvet coat thing. It was sleeveless so his huge, fancy sleeves showed.

"Are you ready?" He asked.

"Yep. Let's get this over with. I can't imagine how people wore this stuff all the time, especially in the summer."

As they stepped outside, Rachel was once more half hoping the whole thing had stopped and that she was going to be faced with big red London buses and black cabs. Her heart sank a little when that dirt track appeared along with those grazing horses in the fields opposite.

Peter locked the door and shoved the keys in the draw string purse that hung at his waist. He held out his arm and she took it, slipped her little finger into the loop on her skirt and they began their walk towards the Tower of London.

Nobody stared at them now; no overdressed noblemen drew rein to chastise or threaten and Rachel began to relax.

Most of the area consisted of thatched barns that had been turned into shops of a kind. There were men and women standing outside some of these shops, inviting passers by inside as they had no windows in which to display their goods.

"Shame they don't take credit cards," Rachel whispered to her companion. "I'd love to have a look in some of these places."

"Geez, Rache, you haven't brought any with you, have you?"

"Of course not. I was only joking."

He laughed, drawing the attention of a woman hawking her goods beside a barn.

"Come inside, My Lord," she said. "I've lots of pretty things for your lady."

He shook his head and walked a little faster, wanting to avoid interacting with anyone here.

The slightest thing could change history and he wondered if Rachel had thought of that. But she must have, surely; she was an intelligent woman after all.

"Why did she call you 'my lord'?" Rachel asked.

"Because of the clothes. I think that only the nobility wore this sort of stuff; no one else was allowed to."

She shook her head, wondering how anyone could live like that.

They walked on, getting closer to the gates of London and as they did so, the streets got busier. Now there were cobblestones beneath their feet instead of dirt, the shopfronts were proper buildings and some had actual glass in the windows, leaded and dark so not much could be seen. There were a lot more horses and more of those funny old wooden carriages with the huge wheels that bumped over the cobblestones.

Rachel wondered how anyone could travel in them; it would be like being on a fairground ride. God help anyone with a bad back.

Peter stopped abruptly, making Rachel trip over her skirt. She looked at him with a frown of irritation, only to see he was staring into the distance at a massive church. She didn't recognise it, but she knew the area.

"It's St Paul's Cathedral," he said. "St. Paul's

before the fire."

"It's beautiful," Rachel replied.

She found herself staring at it as well, even though she had little real interest in history and certainly none in religion. But this was a sight she could never see in her own time, the original medieval cathedral with spires and carvings which must have taken years to build. And it took one small fire in a baker's shop to destroy it completely.

"Come on." She pulled at his arm to make him move. "We don't want to be still wandering about in the dark, do we?"

They walked on in silence, watching the people in their strange costumes. There were one or two dressed like them, but all had servants running along behind them. The ladies didn't bother holding up their skirts like Rachel; they had little girls to do that. They were there to hold up their trains.

"Some of those girls don't look more than about eight," Rachel remarked.

"They're probably not. They didn't have any laws about child labour."

Something else which upset Rachel and made her wish she had some money was the sight of children, skinny and filthy children, sitting and begging at the side of the road.

The smell hit them before they saw where it

was coming from.

"Oh, my God!" Rachel cried out. "What the hell is that?"

Her loud voice made a few people turn and frown at her and she realised she wasn't behaving very ladylike, but this stench was intolerable. She looked around, trying to recognise the area in which they now found themselves, but there were very few familiar buildings.

They seemed to be the only nobility who were walking here. There were carriages that picked up speed as they made their way through this area, but the only people walking were very poorly dressed and very dirty. Some were even barefoot.

"We have to go this way," Peter said. "I don't want to get lost."

She lifted her arm and pressed her sleeve against her nose, but it did little good and at last they came to the source of the stink, Newgate Prison, and as they hurried past it, they saw that the shops close by were all tightly shut.

"Why does it stink so badly?" Rachel asked.

"Because in Newgate Prison nothing was provided that wasn't paid for. That included the removal of human waste or even corpses." Peter covered his mouth in an attempt to control his heaving stomach. "Let's get out of here, Rache, before I lose my breakfast."

He caught her hand and they ran, no longer caring if anyone thought their behaviour strange, until the disgusting stench of Newgate Prison no longer lingered in the air. They stopped at a little green and sank down onto the grass, attracting a few curious glances but nothing more.

Rachel breathed in the fresh air and realised just how fresh it was. There were still smells in the air, unpleasant smells, but so entirely different to their own London air, polluted by exhaust fumes.

"You do realise, Pete," she said, "that we've got to go back that way."

"Perhaps we can find a carriage for hire or something."

"What with? We've only got one coin and you wouldn't want to part with that."

"No, but you might be able to bribe someone with that fancy necklace. I'm sure those rubies are real."

"Anyway," she said, pushing herself up, "it looks like we're here."

His eyes followed hers and he scrambled to his feet and brushed the grass off his coat. There it stood, majestic and not much different to how it looked today.

"No drainpipes," he remarked.

"What?"

"No drainpipes," he repeated. "The Tower has drainpipes in our time, and guttering, but not here. Nothing to spoil the view. It's even got a moat."

"And look what's being dumped into it," Rachel said as they walked toward the ancient building.

Something was sliding down the wall, something unsavoury and very smelly.

"You just had to spoil it, didn't you?" he asked with a grin.

As they got closer they could see into the Tower grounds, could see the green where the princes were reputed to have been seen playing before they disappeared. It was quiet and empty, no sign of anyone, not even a beefeater.

"How do you suppose we are going to get inside?" Rachel asked.

"From what I've read, the Tower in the fifteenth century wasn't just a prison; it was also a residence of a kind. It was fairly open really; anyone could come and go and it was only the cells themselves that were locked up."

"You're willing to risk your life on that, are you? And mine."

"I'm sure I'm right. The princes were never imprisoned here, they were housed here, first in the royal apartments then in a chamber in the middle tower and that was only because Richard needed the royal apartments for his own coronation." She raised her eyebrows sceptically. "We should be able to go inside unchallenged."

"Well, you're on your own," Rachel said. "I'm staying put."

She sat down on the grass outside the wall and leaned back.

"You can't stay there on your own," Peter argued. "Supposing someone sees you."

"So what?"

"You are supposed to be a noblewoman, a fifteenth century noblewoman who wouldn't be seen on the streets alone, never mind squatting down on the grass."

"Well, you'd better not be long then."

His mind was busy with a suitable retort when there was movement on the green and he turned quickly to see the princes, just as those artists of old imagined them. But they weren't alone; there were two yeoman guards carefully watching.

"Beefeaters," Rachel said.

She had got up from her inelegant position and was peering over the wall beside him.

"Yes, that's what we call them, but they weren't curious tourist attractions here. They were yeomen of the guard and extremely dangerous."

They watched from a crouching position, just their eyes peering over the wall and hoped these medieval yeomen of the guard didn't see them. The younger boy was kicking a ball about the green, but the older one sat on a stone bench and was busy writing on a scroll of parchment. He'd even got a pot of ink and a quill pen, so obviously this was no clandestine occupation.

After about ten minutes and what looked like a lot of script, the young King set aside his writing materials and got up to play some sort of football with his brother.

"The young King," whispered Peter. "We are actually looking at King Edward V."

"It's exciting, isn't it?" Rachel replied. "I have to say it feels like a dream."

"It does, but it isn't a dream and we must be very careful."

They watched in silence for about an hour more before the princes followed the guards back inside the Tower.

"They don't appear to be prisoners," said Rachel.

"They never were. This must be the period when they were housed in the royal apartments waiting for the coronation. They won't be disappearing for a long time yet."

"Well, I'm certainly not sticking around until they do."

"No, that wouldn't be very practical, would it?"

He watched for a little while longer, hoping to catch another glimpse of these mysterious boys, but nobody reappeared. His eyes wandered to the bench where the young King had been writing and he grabbed Rachel's wrist so tightly she struggled and cried out.

"Get off, Pete! You're hurting me."

"Sorry," he said as he released her. "Look; Edward's left his scroll behind."

"His what?"

"His scroll, what he was writing."

He scrambled up the wall, thankful for his sessions at the local gym, and raced to the bench. Grabbing the scroll, trying hard not to squash it, he ran back to Rachel, climbed over the wall and turned to be sure he wasn't seen.

"What is it?" She asked.

"I don't know, but it was important enough for him to be spending precious play time writing it. It could be a journal, a diary of some sort."

"Then why have we never heard of it? Or have we?"

"No, but that could be because it incriminated someone, so it was destroyed."

"Or it could be because you stole it."

He could only stare at her, wondering if she

was right. He had no idea how it would work. It was a bit like the old adage of going back in time and killing your own grandfather; a paradox.

"Come on," he said. "We need to get back before it gets dark. I don't much fancy hanging around these streets at night."

He stuffed the scroll into the front of his jacket and they began to walk quickly back toward Holborn and the curious antique shop.

They had gone only a few hundred yards when Rachel spotted a jeweller's shop. It wasn't easy to detect from all the other rickety wooden buildings, but it had a big sign outside declaring its trade.

"Let's go in there," she said, her arms up to unclasp the ruby necklace that adorned her neck. "We can see if they'll buy this for enough to hire us a ride. I don't fancy walking past that stinking prison again."

The shopkeeper gave them a huge smile, no doubt hoping they were going to spend lots of money. If only he knew how broke they were. There was an old oak table along one wall and Rachel placed the necklace carefully on its rough surface.

"We want to sell this," she said.

The shopkeeper frowned at her, then turned to Peter.

"Is that your wish, My Lord?" he said.

Rachel felt her anger growing like a high wind that grew in fury until it swept away trees and vehicles alike.

"It's my bloody necklace!" she shouted.

Peter put his arm around her and hugged her gently, then smiled at the shopkeeper.

"You must forgive my wife," he said. "She is rather outspoken, for a woman."

He could almost feel her glare burning into him, but he couldn't afford to worry about offending her feminist sensibilities.

"My Lord," said the shopkeeper with a bow. "You wish to sell this necklace? It is rather beautiful, and I can see the rubies are genuine."

Then he named a price, leaving Peter and Rachel at a loss to know whether it was a good price or not. Neither knew anything about the value of the contemporary money, and they had no choice but to accept. When the man brought out a gold coin, similar to the one in Peter's pocket but with Edward IV engraved around the edge, they thought they had done well.

"Now, Sir," Peter said, not sure whether a lord would address a shopkeeper as 'sir', "Is there somewhere we can hire a carriage and driver to take us to Holborn?"

He wasn't at all sure that Holborn was called Holborn in the fifteenth century, but the shopkeeper seemed to know where he meant.

"My son, My Lord, will drive you for a price."

The man led them to a door at the back of the shop where a young man sat on a tree stump beside one of those peculiar wooden carriages. They climbed inside and sat down on the hard wooden benches.

"I'm going to get a splinter in my bits by the time we get there," said Peter.

"Better than walking past that stink."

By the end of the journey, they were not sure she spoke the truth.

***

"Can we go home, Peter?" Rachel was saying. "We can go back to my place and you can study that thing to your heart's content."

"Do you think so?" he said. "I'm betting I can't remove it from this shop without taking it back to its own time, just like everything else."

"Well, yes, you might be right, but I'm starving. We forgot to take sandwiches on our little adventure, didn't we?"

He got up, now changed into his tee shirt and jeans, and with the scroll in his hand. He opened the front door and looked across the dirt track to the fields opposite, then he opened the door wider so that Rachel could see.

"Well, I'm not staying here all night," she

said. "It'll take you ages to decipher that writing. Lock it in the back room with the other stuff and we can start again in the morning."

"I shan't be able to sleep."

"I will. I'm exhausted after that long walk and that coach ride was even worse. I thought my spine was going to crack. I need a nice, hot, soothing bath."

There was a lot more to the scroll than Peter had imagined. It seemed the young King had been writing it since his father died, possibly even longer, and he knew Rachel was right; this would take a long time to decipher and he was thankful he'd had some training in reading ancient documents.

"Ok," he said. "We'll get some dinner on the way back. Can I stay at yours tonight?"

"Again? The neighbours'll get the wrong idea."

"Look, you want to stay in your aunts' house, don't you? Rent me a couple of rooms."

"I had thought of asking."

"Good. It'll be great, won't it? We can talk about this, together. I can't go back to my place and keep quiet or even try to explain to those junkie pillocks."

"Ok," she said. "I'll rent you a couple of rooms but I still might have to sell the house sooner rather than later. The council tax alone will be astronomical, and it'll cost a fortune to heat the place." She paused thoughtfully. "And I've a feeling it's worth a few million."

He waved the scroll at her.

"So will this be if we can somehow get it into the twenty first century."

"Bury it," Rachel said.

"What?"

"Bury it," she repeated. "Or hide it somewhere. Take it outside and hide it, then we can dig it up in our time and say we just found it."

He stared at her, his mouth hanging open unattractively.

"That's brilliant," he said. "All these years I've known you, and I had no idea you had such a high functioning brain."

"I'm glad you like it."

"I do; I like it a lot, but can you think of somewhere, anywhere, I can bury this scroll, where I might still be able to find it six hundred years later, in the twenty first century?"

CHAPTER FIVE
The Hiding Place

After spending another night on Rachel's sofa, which didn't invite sleep at the best of times, Peter's mind was too busy to do more than doze for a few hours. He got up at four o'clock in the morning, made himself some coffee and thought about the scroll.

He considered Rachel's idea that it had never emerged because he took it and wondered if he ought to put it back. But he'd read it first, make sure there was nothing written there that could threaten Richard III or anyone else. He was quite certain that if it turned out to be inflammatory, it would be destroyed.

They had to park in the underground car park near the shop the following day. There was nowhere on the street to park on a weekday and who knew how long they'd be gone? But the car parks in London cost a fortune, and if they had to do that every day, Rachel would need to sell the house just to pay for it.

One thing that puzzled Peter had been the passage of time; would they return to the antique shop at the same moment they had left it? Or would time pass in the same manner as it had in the past?

He read some of the scroll before they left, before they stepped out of the front door and onto the dirt track of fifteenth century Holborn.

It appeared to be a journal, a journal that began with the death of King Edward IV and carried on through the young King's escort to London and to the royal apartments in the Tower.

It spoke of young Edward's faith in his uncle.

My uncle has brought my young brother, Richard, to keep me company and to attend me at my coronation. I confess the prospect unnerves me somewhat; I expected to be a grown man before I succeeded my beloved father and I've had little time to mourn him.

I know my uncle has gone to a great deal of effort to be sure I reach my coronation unharmed, to fulfil his promise to my father and I am shocked that those I thought my friends proved to be traitors.

I only wish I could see my mother.

This was only a small part of Peter's translation and he had to find a way to bring it into his own time, so that he could translate and publish the entire document. If he interpreted this part correctly, it seemed the young King had accepted Richard of York's charge against his mother's brother, Lord Rivers, and his own half brother.

It was always assumed by opponents of Richard that young King Edward had no say in the matter, but this seemed to prove otherwise. Perhaps those Ricardians, those supporters of King Richard III, were right after all. Who knew? Peter hoped further study of the journal would tell him.

Dressed up in their fifteenth century garb, Rachel and Peter took the journal outside once more.

"It's really too warm for this stuff," Rachel complained. "How could they walk about in silk and velvet in seventy degrees?"

But there was something about the air here. It was still warm, just like any English summer could be when it felt like it, but it was cleaner somehow, more breathable. There were smells, certainly, the smells of horse manure left in the street, and nobody was walking behind their dogs with little plastic poo bags either. In fact the dogs were running free, often alone and taking themselves for a walk.

As the couple got closer to the city gates, the smell of rancid food and human waste grew stronger and hardly bearable.

"I wish I'd brought my fresh air spray," she said.

"That wouldn't have looked conspicuous now, would it?"

"It's no good, Pete. We'll never find anywhere to hide the journal here, nowhere where we'll be able to find it again at any rate. All this is paved over or built on; we'll have to go out to the countryside, one of those old churches perhaps."

He stopped walking and turned to look at her thoughtfully.

"I knew I was right in bringing you. I'd never have managed without your counsel, my dear."

"Ok, here's a thought. We go back to our own time, drive out to one of the villages, perhaps in Essex or Surrey, somewhere not too far from London. We can talk to the locals, find out how old their church is. Some of them are nearly a thousand years old."

"How come you know that?"

"Because I'm not blind."

As they turned to walk back toward the shop, they realised they had attracted an audience. Apparently, lords and ladies of the nobility did not stand about arguing in the street.

A man approached, a lavishly dressed gentleman in satin and gold thread. His eyes wandered over Rachel and he grimaced, making her wonder if she had something on her face that shouldn't have been there.

"Is there some trouble with your wife, My Lord?" He said. "Do you need some assistance?"

Rachel's mouth opened, the words of protest

hammering on her tongue to get out, but Peter gripped her upper arm so tightly she winced.

"Not at all, My Lord," he said. "Just a difference of opinion."

"In public? She cannot be allowed to disrespect you in public, Sir." The man drew himself up, straightened stiffly so as to appear taller. "I would not allow it in private, but that is your concern."

"Yes, it is," Peter replied.

It was clear that even he, with his easy going attitude to life, was beginning to lose patience with this interference from complete strangers. He loosened his grip on her arm and turned her away and back towards the antique shop.

"That hurt," she muttered, rubbing her arm before slipping a hand in the bend of his elbow and walking quickly beside him.

"Sorry, love, but I had to keep your mouth shut somehow. I knew what you were about to say, and I have a feeling that bloke was someone who would cause trouble. We can't afford that; we need to get that journal out of London."

"There's an old church near here," Rachel said. "It's the oldest Catholic church in England, built in the seventh century."

"And it's still squashed into London. We need somewhere outside, somewhere quiet where we might be able to hide it in a place that'll still be there in the twenty first century. Churches would be ideal, but there's the dissolution, the reformation when they pulled all the shrines apart."

They changed clothes in the back room, something Rachel was getting a little tired of. It wouldn't be so bad if these medieval clothes weren't so complicated.

Peter straightened up, zipped up his jeans and placed the scroll carefully in the drawer with the coins and necklaces.

"We'll go back to your place and find a map."

"I'm not getting much work done like this, am I?" Rachel said. "Neither are you. Don't the museum expect you to go in today?"

"Nope. I rang them and claimed some of my long overdue holiday. What about you?"

"I'm supposed to be working at home this week. If this goes all right, I'll be chucking that job. I'm sick of coming up with great designs only to have him claim credit for them."

"I don't blame you."

"And I haven't even looked at the house yet," she said. "We've been so wrapped up in this time slip business, we haven't even been inside."

"She didn't have a cat or anything, did she?"

"No," she said, shaking her head impatiently. "I would never forget something like that. But it's possible there might be some sort of record there, some notes my uncle wrote that'll tell us more."

"Good thinking, Batman," he answered. "We'll drive out and find a village with an ancient church, see if we can find somewhere to hide this, then we can get it sorted and explore the house."

***

The church was old all right, but it was difficult to tell how old. It was one of those quaint places with cobblestones embedded in the walls, one of those buildings that makes one wonder how they had stayed up all these centuries.

Beside it was a huge house, almost as big as the church itself. Above the door was a sign declaring it to be the Rectory. They used to house the rector or vicar in houses like this, when the church considered them to be very important people. Nowadays they were lucky to get a three bed semi on a housing estate, but these houses were still named as rectories or vicarages.

They walked around the little churchyard, carefully studying the graves to see how old they were, but the oldest they found was eighteenth century.

"There are never graves much older than that," Rachel said.

"How do you know?"

"Because I like nosing round graveyards, that's how. Just because the graves don't go back that far, doesn't mean the church doesn't. We need to find the vicar."

"Did I hear my name?" said a quiet voice behind them.

They turned to see a tall man, around sixty, with a shock of almost white hair and a collar declaring him to be the vicar of this parish. They felt as though they'd been caught out doing something illegal and their nervous smiles must have told the man that they weren't accustomed to consecrated ground.

"I'm Philip Smithson," said the vicar.

He held out his hand and first Rachel, then Peter shook it, as they introduced themselves and asked their question.

"Why, the church itself goes back to the twelfth century," Philip said. "Of course, it was Catholic then and it had a famous shrine before King Henry vandalised it."

"But the rest? I mean the stones, the pews, the churchyard?"

"Oh, yes, it's all as it was. Of course the graves from back then have all disintegrated or been re-used."

"Re-used?"

"Yes. Most of the graves were public; that's all these poor people could afford and they're re-used after a century. The only tombs that still remain from that time are in the crypt.

Peter made no reply. There were some stone mausoleums dotted here and there which would suit their purpose wonderfully, but he wasn't sure how old they were.

"What about the mausoleums?" he asked.

"They are mostly Victorian or later," said Reverend Smithson. "The very oldest are, as I said, in the crypt."

"How do we get to that?"

The Reverend stiffened, Rachel shook her head despairingly.

"I'm afraid you don't, young man. The crypt was only ever opened to receive the newly departed of the ruling family here. Since they have all died out, it is sealed up."

"You must forgive him, Reverend," Rachel said. "He gets carried away with his love of history."

"I quite understand, Miss," he replied with a forced smile. "The oldest grave in the churchyard is in the far corner beside the wall. Legend has it that it contains the remains of a child whose mother murdered her, before taking her own life."

"When was that?"

"Oh, let me see, it was during the wars. I believe Henry VI was on the throne, you know the mad King of the Lancastrian cause. It was something to do with him, I think. The mother was the widow of a Yorkist soldier and lost everything when he was defeated in battle. Very sad times." He paused and shook his head slowly. "Of course, there is no marker there, not any longer. I'm not sure there ever was."

"Thank you, Reverend," Rachel said quickly, before Peter could ask more embarrassing questions.

They spent another hour or so, wandering around the churchyard and the village, hoping to find somewhere else that might be safe to hide the journal. They considered the village green, the earth near the church walls, even some of the narrow lanes that were still dirt.

"I wonder if there's any way into the crypt besides through the church," Peter muttered, more to himself than to her.

"No. Not only will we get caught, but I'm not going down there with all those coffins."

"It'll be an ideal hiding place."

"Maybe, but if you want to do that, you're on your own."

CHAPTER SIX
Desecration

"First we need to sell some more of the jewellery," said Peter. "We'll sell a few more rings and necklaces, find a jewellers or a pawn shop or something."

"We could go back to the one where we sold the necklace."

"No," Peter said. "He's already suspicious. You know, I knew women were chattels, but I didn't realise how subservient they were supposed to be in public."

"Well, you'd better brush up on it then. I can't guarantee to keep quiet for their insults."

"You'd better, Rachel," he said. "I think an insolent woman leaves herself open to all sorts."

"Ok," Rachel answered. "But how are we going to get there? I hope you don't think I'm going to walk all the way to Ongar."

"Ever ridden a horse?"

"No, and I'm not about to start now. I don't fancy driving something with a mind of its own."

"It's ok. First we find somewhere to sell the necklace. Then we find somewhere that rents out carriages, complete with driver, and we pay him to take us to Ongar. We dig up where that child's grave is, slip the journal inside, come back here, change, then drive back to Ongar and retrieve it. Simple."

It sounded it, certainly, but Rachel thought it sounded a bit too simple. Anything could go wrong, and probably would.

"What are we going to put it in?" she said.

"What?"

"The scroll. We can't just shove it in the earth, can we? It'll disintegrate. I've got some Tupperware at home, but it was guaranteed for ten years not six hundred."

"You've done it again, haven't you?"

"Done what?"

"Thought of something that would never have occurred to me until we got there. I just wish you'd done it before we left your flat. I need something to put the journal in, something imperishable, like glass. I don't suppose there's anything here, is there?" He moved back into the main shop and began to hunt about for some sort of container. "Please don't tell me we've got to change out of this lot again."

He stared down at his elaborate medieval clothes, then looked hopefully at Rachel.

"There's a flask in my car," she said.

"Really? That's great. There's not many people about and if anyone notices, they'll think you're going to a costume party or something."

She nodded, picked up her car keys then opened the door.

"What's wrong?"

"I can't get out, not wearing this lot anyway."

"Oh, bugger," he muttered. "I forgot about that."

Rachel went to the counter, the one in the front of the shop with the long gloves and other items that had actually been for sale in this place. She pulled out the drawers, lifting out the contents and studying them.

"Leather?" she asked, waving a long glove in the air.

"No. It'll never last."

"Hang on," she said. On one of the high shelves behind the counter, she spotted a dried flower arrangement inside a glass jar, one of those hideous Victorian affairs. "If we can get the flowers out of this, we might be able to use it."

Once they had pulled out the glass stopper, they found the mouth of the jar wide enough to pull out the flowers.

"This is ideal, Rache," Peter said. "It's even got a lid."

He rolled the scroll as tightly as he dared, terrified of damaging it, and pushed it inside the jar, fitting the stopper in tightly. This glass jar had to keep its contents safe for six hundred years.

***

The jeweller gave them a good price for the jewels and after the suspicion they'd caused last time, Rachel agreed to keep her mouth shut. At least they thought it was a good price; there was no way of telling really, but it was more than enough to hire a carriage and coachman to take them out to Ongar and to the little church of St Mary Magdalene, where they had planned to hide the jar containing the scroll.

"Wait here, coachman, please," Peter ordered as he climbed down, helped Rachel down after him and closed the door. "We have to pay our respects to our ancestors."

He offered Rachel his arm and she took it, feeling just as silly now as she had at the beginning of this adventure. All looked much as it had in their own time and they walked as sedately as their patience would allow to the back of the ancient building.

Peter moved away from her and began to survey the little churchyard, wondering how far down he'd have to dig to preserve the journal and get it into the twenty first century.

"That wall looks very much the same," said Rachel.

She hastened to the corner of the churchyard, looking down at her feet to avoid treading in something unsavoury. Nobody seemed to clear up after their dogs in this century and she was sure there were a few piles of human waste that she had no wish to encounter.

There was a small grave in the corner, right up against the wall. It had no stone, just a plain wooden cross whose inscription had long since faded. She turned to Peter, who still stood looking around hopefully.

"Here, Pete," she called out. "This must be the one the vicar told us about. Poor little soul. Bring the jar."

She'd brought a little garden trowel as it was easy to hide, and was digging into the earth at the corner, beside the stone wall when he arrived, and had dug a hole deep enough to contain the jar and hold its secret into the future. At least, they could only hope so.

He knelt down and pushed the jar as deep into the earth as he could, his leggings stained with wet, black soil. He got to his feet, reached out a hand to help Rachel to hers and began to brush down his hose.

"Now all we need do is go back, drive out here and hope no one's found it."

"If they have, we'll soon find out. There will be a record of it somewhere."

But their journey was to take longer than they expected.

"Sacrilege! Desecration!" came a terrified voice from the lychgate.

They hadn't thought to hide their actions from the waiting coachman, who had an excellent view from his position high up in the driver's seat of his coach. Now he was striding angrily toward them, all thoughts of deference for their supposed status having fled.

They hurried toward him, hoping there was something they could say to allay his fear, or something they could give to bribe him into silence.

"No, my man," said Peter. "We were but paying our respects."

"I saw you," said the angry and terrified coachman. "Tis well known that grave belongs to a little girl who was murdered by her own mother. I saw you digging there, taking the earth."

Rachel almost laughed, but stopped herself quickly when she realised it would not be wise.

"What would we want with earth from a grave?" Peter said.

"Everyone knows tis the most powerful for making spells. You two ain't no lord and lady; you are witches."

"No," said Peter. "No, we are not witches. We

came to pay our respects to the child, to pray for her to ease her soul through purgatory."

Peter paused, hoping he had his dates right and this was not too early. The church dreamed up purgatory at some point, but he couldn't remember when.

"Drive us back to London," Rachel said quickly. "We've got a lot of money, Sir. We can pay well."

The man scoffed.

"And why would you want to do that, My Lady," he said, "if you have nothing to hide? Father Matthew's already gone for the constable."

Peter decided there was no point in standing about arguing with the coachman, when any minute now the priest would be back with who knew what sort of law enforcement. He caught Rachel's hand and ran with her, past the spot where the angry coachman stood, almost breathing self righteousness.

But as they reached the lychgate, the priest caught up with them and grabbed the back of Peter's velvet mantle, pulling him back just as two other men arrived on the scene.

There was no chance now of escaping back to London.

***

It was a dungeon, a genuine, medieval dungeon, complete with manacles hanging by chains from the stone walls. It even had damp shining on those walls and a little wooden bench that was the only source of comfort. The door was rotting wood, blackened by ages of damp and Peter was just tall enough to see through the tiny barred opening in that door.

"You'll stay here," said one of the constables.

He seemed fearful rather than angry, as though he could not wait to lock the door and be done with his troublesome prisoners. Peter wondered if the silly man thought they could cast a spell on him and if they could, they wouldn't be here, would they?

"How long do we have to stay here?" Peter demanded. "We have done nothing."

"You're witches," he replied. "You'll hang most likely, but the Lord has to decide on that."

"The Lord?" said Rachel with a snigger. "You mean God?"

The constable took a step back and away from the door.

"You take the Lord's name in vain," he said. "God will strike you down."

"I only asked a civil question," Rachel replied. "Which Lord were you talking about?"

"I think he means me," said a new voice.

The constable bowed, stepped back even further to make room for a tall, handsome man wearing those fancy fabrics Peter had told her about, fabrics like the stuff they wore themselves. Only this one was a real Lord, not a fake one like Peter.

"I am the Earl of Chadwin," he said. "I am the Lord of this manor and your fate is in my hands."

"Don't we get a trial?" Rachel demanded.

The Earl frowned, scrutinised her with velvet brown eyes while his mouth formed an angry line.

"Is this your wife?" He directed his question at Peter.

"She is, My Lord."

"Then keep her under control."

"How..." Rachel began, but Peter again gripped her arm to silence her.

"Be quiet, Rachel," he said. "Allow me to deal with this."

She was furious both with him and this pompous earl who thought he could tell her how to behave. But she was in no position to argue; she would save her fury for when they got home; if they got home.

"My Lord," Peter said, stepping in front of Rachel. "We have been falsely accused."

"I am told you are witches, that you were

seen taking earth from a grave in the churchyard, the grave of a murdered child. What explanation do you have for that?"

"We were not taking earth, My Lord," Peter replied. "We were merely paying our respects."

"Why? The child was an orphan; you are not relatives."

"We wanted to be sure we said prayers for her soul."

"Would it not be more appropriate to have masses said?"

Rachel tried to push her way in front, longing to say her piece, but still Peter pushed her back.

"My Lord," Peter said in an assertive voice, the one he used on shop keepers who refused to give him a refund. "We have little in the way of funds. We thought we could say our own prayers."

"That then, Sir, is blasphemy."

He turned to go, but Peter thought of something else.

"My Lord!" he called after him. "If we took earth from the grave, where is it?"

The Earl turned back to stare at him thoughtfully.

"I imagine you dropped it back into the grave when the coachman shouted. Tis what I would have done."

Peter watched him go then turned to his

companion, to be met with a punch to his chest. He caught her wrist, led her to the little bench and pulled her to sit beside him. She was shaking, her whole body trembling and he knew that was her reason for lashing out as she had.

"Rachel, calm down, sweetheart," he said. "We're not dead yet."

"It won't be long though, will it? I should never have listened to you. I should have set a match to that bloody shop and claimed on the insurance. That's the best use for it and it's what'll happen if we ever get back, though that's looking less and less likely."

He pulled her into his arms, hoped he could keep his own trembling under control long enough to soothe hers. This was an eventuality he had not considered, and he had no idea how he was going to get them out of it. If truth be told, he was just as scared as she was, but he wasn't about to tell her that.

Judging by the few glimpses of attitudes to women they had so far seen, Peter understood how it was always the man who was expected to rescue the female from disaster. Throughout history they had taken it upon themselves to be in charge, so they thought it their responsibility to protect the woman. In Peter and Rachel's time, attitudes had changed, but even so he felt compelled to comfort her.

"How are we going to get out of this, Pete?" Rachel asked.

"I'll think of something."

"What?"

"I don't know," he said with a shrug. "Something."

"Seems to me you've already thought of enough," she said bitterly. "Look where we are. All because you wanted to see the princes."

He retreated into a thoughtful silence for a few minutes. It was possible that if people were concerned with the coronation and the whereabouts of the young King and his brother, they might not have time to worry about a couple of witches. This earl would be duty bound to attend the ceremony after all. It was a possibility, a slim one, but he wouldn't tell Rachel and build her hopes.

It was June when the princes were last seen, playing on that same green where Peter and Rachel had seen them. Shortly after, they had disappeared from public view into the middle tower and in July, their uncle had them declared illegitimate and himself crowned King Richard III.

That's all Peter remembered, but time seemed to move at the same pace as it did for them in their own time. It had been only a few days since they'd watched the princes; it would be a long time before they vanished.

Someone was at the door, turning the lock and Peter stood up. He had a vague idea that he might be able to overcome the guard and if he could, they'd be able to escape. But there were two guards and the one behind held a sword to protect the one in front and keep the prisoners in their place.

"You," the first guard said, while the second one pointed his sword at Peter. "Come with me."

"Where to?"

"You say you are not witches," he replied with a cynical smile. "Now is your chance to prove it."

One guard bent and pulled Peter to his feet and out of the cell, leaving Rachel to stare after them. They took him deeper into the bowels of the castle and into a room very like the cell he had just left.

He was terrified, but he wasn't about to let them know it. They thought he was a witch; it was likely he would be tied to a ducking stool, the most ridiculous idea ever invented by a people who believed that every thought that entered their head was God's word, that He was talking to them.

He had come here thinking it would be educational, and it was definitely that, but never being able to get home again was not something he had considered. And he had the coin; he didn't know if Rachel could get back without it.

It was dark in here. There were no windows at all, no light except one stinking tallow candle on a table in the centre of the room. Seated at the table was the Earl they had met earlier and he dismissed the guards and pointed Peter toward a chair.

"The guards will expect you to be swum, to see whether the Devil protects you. I have a better idea."

"What?"

"You have a beautiful wife," he said. "I could be lenient in exchange for a few hours of her company."

Peter wanted to laugh. The very idea of Rachel complying with that idea was funny, or would be under any other circumstances. In all his education about the history of England, he had never read that it was usual for a man to lend his wife to another man for any reason. If anything, they were protective to the point of controlling.

"My wife's body, Sir," said Peter, "belongs to her. If you want to know her better, you had better ask her."

Lord Chadwin smiled.

"Of course," he said. "I wanted to be sure you

are agreeable."

Peter sighed. He was getting angry now and they hadn't put manacles on him, as he would have expected. He could leap across the table and break this man's neck with one, well placed Karate blow. After years of training, it could be the first and only time he could make use of that black belt.

But he was aware of the danger of changing history. This man could have children, and one of those children could grow up to invent the train, or the aircraft. One of those children might be his own ancestor.

"Of course I'm not agreeable," Peter said. "She is my wife, my property not yours, and besides, I love her."

"Love?" The Earl was shaking his head slowly, grinning sardonically. "That is not something I have encountered. Guard!"

Peter turned his head to see the door opening and one of the guards coming back in. He stood up.

"Take him back to his cell," he said.

Peter did not know whether to be relieved or wary of what else this man had in store for them. He might have to use his skills to get them out of this.

The guard pushed him into the cell and he stumbled toward Rachel, where she sat on that little wooden bench, worrying. She leapt to her feet and into his arms, clutching him so tight he thought his bones would crack.

"It's all right, love," he said. "I'm still in one piece."

"What happened? Did you clobber that self important earl?"

"I was tempted but I can't be sure he doesn't have children that could change history. We have to be careful."

"To hell with that," she said. "I'm cold, I'm hungry and I'm filthy. I need a big mug of hot chocolate and a cigarette."

"You don't smoke."

"I used to. This is just the sort of experience to make me start again."

Then the door opened again and they turned.

The first guard carried a tray which held a metal bowl, a bit like a dog's bowl only not stainless steel and this one was battered and dented.

He brought the tray into the cell and set it down on the bench beside Peter.

"Only one of us can eat?" Peter said.

He squinted at the watery porridge that seemed to be all there was in the bowl. There was nothing else, no bread, nothing.

"His Lordship wishes the lady to join him for dinner," said the guard.

"What?" Rachel was startled. "I'd rather starve."

Peter lowered his voice to a whisper and drew close so that only she could hear.

"Use your noddle, Rache," he said. "You can work your charms on him. He's likely never seen a woman as clean as you; you might be able to get us out."

He didn't want to tell her of the Earl's earlier proposition. He thought it would only put her back up and besides, she could look after herself, just as long as she didn't kill him.

She glared at him angrily. What he said made sense and the Earl had been a good looking man. She was a liberated woman from the twenty first century, not some innocent virgin who knew nothing, and if she could use her womanly wiles to free them both, why not? But it would be a last resort.

"All right," she said grudgingly.

She bent and kissed his cheek before straightening up and following the guards out of the cell. As they walked, she tried her best to remember where she was going so that she could come back later and rescue Peter. But, if she played her cards right, she might not have to. She might be able to persuade this Lord of the Manor to release him in return for favours.

She would have to be careful though. She

knew very little about this era and she had no idea how a woman would behave in this situation. She had a feeling marriages among the nobility were arranged so it should come as no surprise to the Earl that his captive might be willing to betray her husband. She didn't have to pretend to love him, did she?

She left Peter playing about with the unappealing gruel and wondered if he was yet hungry enough to eat it. Dinner, the guard had said. She might be able to sneak something edible up her sleeve for him.

She followed the guard along the dark and damp corridors, shivered at the chill that almost reached out to cling to her.

Upstairs was like a different world. There was oak panelling over some of the walls and beautifully crafted tapestries hung on the ones that were stone. The floors were covered in sweet smelling rushes, hay with wild flowers laid between it and Rachel had to lift up this ridiculously long skirt to avoid gathering the stuff up and dragging it along with her.

The guard stopped just inside the hallway and handed Rachel over to a maidservant who curtseyed briefly before walking away. Rachel assumed she was expected to follow her so she did and while she did, she noticed the servant was wearing similar clothes to the ones in which

Rachel had first ventured out. No wonder that pompous idiot thought she was a servant.

The maid opened the heavy oak door and stood back to let Rachel pass. Her eyes immediately went to the table, laden with food of every different type, swans and fish put back together as they were in life. It crossed her mind that swans in Great Britain were protected in her time, they all belonged to the Queen, every one of them. It was a crime to kill a swan, never mind eat one.

There was also beef and a huge pig's head as well as vegetables in abundance. She looked for the potatoes, but was disappointed to find there were none. A meal like this needed roast potatoes, but she wouldn't mention it. She wouldn't mention anything that might make the Earl even more convinced that she was a witch.

Seated at the head of the table was the Earl, his legs crossed casually and sipping from what looked like a silver goblet. He stood and held out his hand to her.

"Come," he said. "Eat. You must be hungry."

"Peter is hungry, too," she said.

"Ah, your husband. He was sent food, was he not?"

"Is that what you call it? I wouldn't feed that to my dog."

"You have a dog?"

"No, but you know what I mean. We've done nothing, absolutely nothing. Why are we being treated like criminals?"

"You were disturbing the earth of a grave. That is desecration and could well be construed as witchcraft. The penalty for witchcraft is death."

Rachel felt her cheeks darken, felt them burn and knew they must be giving this man a clear indication of her feelings. She wanted to giggle; the very idea of anyone believing in witchcraft was bizarre, especially not an obviously educated man like the Earl of Chadwin. But then she'd read about satanists who held black masses at midnight in forests. They weren't breaking any laws, though. They weren't being interrogated by some upper class nobleman and held in dungeons, because nobody took them that seriously anymore.

But she was frightened. This man was attractive to be sure, but he was also deadly serious. His eyes were a piercing dark brown and now she felt them boring into her, almost pricking at her skin. Her life was literally in his hands, both their lives were in his hands and she had to do something to bring him over to their side.

"Come," he said. "Sit here and eat, My Lady. I suppose you are entitled to wear the title, are you?"

She sorted through her thoughts, trying to recall what Peter had said. They'd used Attwood, his own name, because it would be easier to remember and he could find no mention of a nobleman with that name ever having existed. So much had happened since then, dragging up the memory almost gave her a headache.

"Attwood," she said abruptly.

"I beg your pardon?"

"Baron and Baroness Attwood."

"I have never heard of you," said the Earl.

That was the idea, thought Rachel as she took a seat beside him at the table.

"No reason why you should have, is there?" she asked. "We come from the north, right next to the Scottish border."

"If you say so," he said.

She was quite convinced he did not believe a word of it and her heart began to hammer ever faster. But the food looked and smelled delicious and she was very hungry. At least there were a lot of vegetables, so she wasn't forced by hunger to eat any of the meat.

When they set out that morning, they had planned to bury the jar with the journal inside, return to London and their own time, then collect her car, drive out to Ongar and dig it up again. The last place they expected to find themselves was in a dungeon in some ancient castle, trying to placate some power crazed, and probably oversexed, Lord of the Manor. She would give a very large chunk of her inheritance for one glimpse of a gorgeous big red bus or black taxi cab.

She began to eat, feeling guilty with every mouthful that brought an image of Peter and his gruel to her mind. He must be cold too. It was freezing in that dungeon and she hoped the clothes he had chosen that morning in the antique shop would keep him warm. But no, they wouldn't would they? He'd chosen them for summer weather, heavier than he'd normally wear, but still not warm enough for that environment.

She looked across at the Earl. He was a lot cleaner than she would have expected. She'd seen television programmes where people from the past were filthy, even the upper classes. She wanted to ask him how often he bathed, but she wouldn't ask that of someone in her own time, so it could hardly be appropriate here.

"Lady Attwood," he murmured. "Do you have a given name?"

"Rachel."

"Ah, very nice. A good biblical name."

Here goes, she thought.

"And you My Lord?"

"Michael," he said. "My name is Michael Sanders, Earl of Chadwin."

She slipped the velvet cloak off her shoulders to reveal the soft flesh beneath. Her cleavage showed above the pearl trimming but Peter had said it was arms that were covered up. How could a man get excited about arms? She leaned forward so that he could see down her front and allowed her hand to cover his.

"Michael," she said softly. "That is a beautiful name, the name of the Archangel."

The Archangel that adorned the coin that had brought them here. She wondered if that was a coincidence, or fate playing a hand.

"It is indeed," he said. "You are very beautiful, Rachel. You are unlike any woman I have ever known."

"How so?"

"You speak your mind, even in public, even when your husband is there to speak for you."

She made no reply for a few minutes, but her anger was rising. Women had fought long and hard for equal rights and now to be singled out because she didn't drop her gaze and keep silent before her man was intolerable.

"I have a brain," she said. "I see no reason not to use it."

He laughed, loudly and joyously, then he

lifted her hand to his lips and kissed it gently. She wanted to pull away; she'd always thought the custom of kissing hands to be a bit peculiar, but obviously this was a regular custom here.

She needed to concentrate on getting herself and her friend back to their own time, whatever it took.

***

The wooden bench was hard and narrow. Peter was afraid to turn over in case he landed on the stone floor among the rat droppings. It was too dark in the cell to see anything, not even his hand in front of his face, and the smells coming from other parts of this underground chamber of horrors made him wretch.

He gave up on sleep, he gave up on resisting the disgusting gruel that was all he would get for his meal. He should have realised something like this might happen; he was the historian. Why didn't it occur to him that they could get into serious trouble? Could it be because he was too arrogant, too excited at the prospect of seeing it all for himself to stop and think about the danger in which he might put himself and Rachel?

He dared not think what might be happening to her. At least she had been invited to share a meal with the Earl, and Peter doubted that meal would consist of gruel. He could only hope she was safe, that this fifteenth century nobleman did not feel himself entitled to force himself on her. After all, he was someone important and she was his prisoner, charged with witchcraft. He might persuade her into his bed with a promise of release, or he might just rape her. He doubted that was considered the crime it was in Peter's time, not when it was a nobleman forcing himself onto a criminal.

But the Earl was a good looking man and if he had been so inclined, Peter would have had no hesitation in offering himself in exchange for release. He had known Rachel well for many years, but their conversation never had gone so deep as to discover if she would do the same.

Still, she could look after herself. The Earl would get the shock of his life he tried to rape Rachel; she was no weak female who would be incapable of fighting him off. She had self defence skills, but she'd never had to use them before.

Peter patted his little purse where the gold coin still resided and thanked God he hadn't been searched. One of the guards might well have stolen the coin, it being solid gold, and he was still not certain whether they would need it to get home.

His back ached from lying on this bench and he was hungry again; one small bowl of watery porridge wasn't enough to feed a grown man. He had a longing for a medium rare fillet steak and wondered if he'd ever taste such a thing again.

He should have known better, should have read up on the actual period instead of thinking he knew it all. He'd been arrogant and too eager to jump in with both feet, and it was his fault they were in this mess. Because of his negligence, they could both end this trip swinging from the end of a rope. And it wouldn't be a modern hanging, either; no trapdoor to open and break your neck, just a long, drawn out choking and in public as well.

He could hear scratching, very loud scratching which he was sure was the noise made by rats. They could be black rats, the ones that had caused the black death. That was just about all he needed, to catch the bloody bubonic plague. It was still rife, had never completely died out after the fourteenth century outbreak that killed millions. Henry VII's father, Edmund Tudor, died of bubonic plague and that was about now, wasn't it?

Suddenly he felt itchy and tried hard to remember the symptoms of the great mortality, as it was often called in its time. He would end up imagining he had it, even if he didn't. He wished he knew what was happening to Rachel. He wished he knew what the Earl had planned for them both. He wished he'd taken more precautions to protect them.

***

Rachel finished what she could eat of the elaborate meal, the vegetables, the fish. She wasn't about to eat swan, especially when it looked so lifelike and the pig's head made her want to throw up.

She still felt guilty, though, filling her stomach while Peter tucked into his bowl of gruel.

"Can we go now, My Lord?" She asked.

"We?"

"My husband and I," she said. "You expect me to sit here and eat while Peter is down in that filthy dungeon with nothing but pigswill for his supper?"

The Earl stood up and reached to take her hand, lifted her to her feet.

"Come," he said. "I wish to show you something."

"What?"

"Come. You will see."

He kept hold of her hand and led her up a stone staircase, along a gallery covered in elaborately woven tapestries and at last to a door, one of those arched wooden doors one saw in castle ruins.

Inside she saw a bed chamber, with more sweet rushes across the floor and a four poster bed which reached to the ceiling. It was high, this bed, with three or four mattresses and a set of wooden steps beside it to aid the sleeper in climbing up.

They reminded her of the wooden steps she had left in the antique shop, jamming open the door ready for their return. Suddenly, she felt very sorry for herself and brushed away the tears that brimmed unexpectedly.

Dammit! She wasn't going to give in to self pity, not when Peter was depending on her to get him out of this. She drew herself up stiffly and turned to face Michael. It was obvious what he wanted, what he expected, and he was an attractive man. She might even give in if he promised to release them both, but she had no idea if she could trust him. Another thought occurred to her; if he was so free with his bed, he was likely suffering from syphilis or some other sexually transmitted disease.

They knew nothing about those things then, did they? And there was no cure for syphilis until Alexander Fleming discovered penicillin. People died from it before then, but not before suffering horrible disfigurement and losing their minds.

This Earl was obviously not that far advanced, and he may well not have the disease at all, but Rachel was taking no chances.

He pulled her into his arms and kissed her, while she stood rigidly and hoped he'd get the message.

"Come, Rachel," he said. "You are accused of witchcraft. I can acquit you of that, your husband too if you wish. All you need do is accommodate me."

She shook her head.

"No. I am faithful to my husband."

"He would want you to do this if it will save his life, will he not?"

"I doubt it, but even so, the decision is mine."

She pushed him away and he stumbled over a footstool behind him. His expression changed to one of fury and he grabbed her arms with vicious force. His strong hand gripped both her wrists and he ripped her bodice at the neckline, leering as he released her breasts.

"Beautiful," he murmured as he pushed her down onto the high bed, lifting her as he did so.

His hand slipped up her leg, lifting her skirt with it and she realised the benefit of all those years of self defence training.

As his mouth came down on her neck, she

remembered the dagger she had seen in a leather sheath attached to his belt. She reached out, seemingly holding her arm around his waist, but instead she pulled out the knife and held it to his throat.

"Get off me," she said.

He stopped what he was doing, then smiled.

"You would not dare," he said.

"You want to count on that, do you?"

She pushed the tip of the knife so that it pierced his neck and he moved back, but she was angry now, angry enough to lash out. She was still wearing her suede shoes, although the soles weren't nearly as strong and heavy as they would be in her own time. Still they were all she had and she needed relief from her rage.

She aimed a kick, pleased to realise that the fancy codpiece was no protection from a well aimed boot. He screamed, clutching his genitals as he fell from the high bed and onto the stone floor. His head bounced against the wall and he clutched the back of it, where blood had begun to trickle down his neck.

Rachel leapt off the bed and backed away from him, although he was in no fit state to attack again.

"That's for all the innocent women you've helped yourself to," she shouted at him. "I don't suppose you've met one before who could fight back."

He made no move to get up. Probably he was still too dizzy from the blow to his head and now Rachel wanted to get out of there before she was charged with murder as well. She had no way of knowing if the bang on his head had fractured his skull and, if it had, if that would be the end of this Earl and his bloodline. She could have changed history; she could get back to her own century to discover everything had changed.

She couldn't worry about that now. She held the dagger out before her, in case he decided to attack again, while her eyes wandered around the chamber to see if there were any other weapons. What she really needed was a gun of some sort, but there didn't seem to be anything like that.

Then she saw it, a sword nestled in a bracket on the wall. She edged toward it, hoping it wasn't too high for her to reach. She'd lose her advantage if she had to climb on something. But she was in luck; it wasn't as high up as it had looked and she lifted it down, surprised at the weight of the thing. However did they manage to fight with these? She promised herself that if she got back, she would book herself into fencing lessons.

She pointed the sword at him now, keeping

the dagger in her left hand. A quick glance at the door told her the key was still in the lock and, keeping her eyes firmly fixed on the Earl, she made her way toward it. Pulling out the key, she opened the door and stepped into the corridor, closing it behind her. She locked it and took the key, pushed it into her bodice as she had nowhere else and, still wielding the sword, she made her way stealthily down the stairs to the ground floor.

It was dark outside now and there was no one about, not even a servant. Rachel supposed people went to bed early in this time; after all, there was no television and reading by candlelight must have been a terrible strain on the eyes.

There was a sickening smell though, a smell of animal fat and it took her a few minutes to realise it was coming from the many candles that stood in iron candlesticks attached to the walls.

She drew a deep breath to control her heaving stomach and opened the door to the underground steps, the ones she had been escorted up earlier that day by a handsome earl and a guard. She lifted the sword, moved it about to make it more comfortable and hoped there was only one guard on duty.

Down these stairs and along these corridors, the light was provided by burning torches in sconces on the walls. The stone was shiny; Rachel reached out and ran her fingers down the wall. It was wet, water actually running down these walls like the condensation sometimes produced by steam. But this wasn't condensation. This was water and it was coming from the filthy moat around this small castle.

She quickened her pace before the castellan escaped from his chamber and came after her. Closer to the cell in which she and Peter had been imprisoned that morning, she heard what sounded like snoring and hoped it was the guard. She also hoped Peter was still there, that they hadn't moved him somewhere else or worse, decided they may as well hang him before the coronation, rather than wait.

Now her heart was hammering, the smoke from the burning torches hurt her eyes and the stink of those animal fat candles could still be smelled from where she was. There were only two doors and propped against the second one was the same guard they'd met that morning. Obviously, they didn't go in for shift work here.

She moved closer and the aroma of body odour joined the smoke and animal fat to assail her nostrils and attack her stomach and her eyes. She'd be sick if she had to stand much more of this.

Reaching the sword out in front of her, she

poked it into the guard's neck to wake him.

"Get up," she demanded.

"Rachel?" Peter's voice came from behind the door and she breathed a sigh of relief. At least he was still alive.

She could just make out his figure, his hands clutching the rusty iron bars in the door, and she poked the guard again, this time much harder.

"I said get up," she repeated.

His eyes opened a little, then they opened wider when he saw the sword and felt it against his neck.

"Open the door," she said. "Now."

He scrambled to his feet and she followed him with the sword, making sure it stayed close to his throat while he pulled the heavy bunch of keys from his belt.

"I fear what His Lordship will say about this," he muttered.

"That's not our problem," Rachel replied. "Now get that door open before I lose my temper."

He obeyed her order, his fingers fumbling in his haste, and the door swung open. Peter stepped out while Rachel prodded the guard with the tip of the sword until he was inside the cell. She locked the door and threw the keys in the corner, so there was no chance that the guard might reach them.

She turned to Peter and he threw his arms around her, hugged her tightly.

"Oh, My God, girl," he said. "I've never been so pleased to see anyone in my life."

CHAPTER SEVEN
The Journey Home

Peter was so tired, he thought he might collapse in a heap before they got away from the castle, but he didn't want Rachel to know that. He didn't know what she'd done to escape from Lord Chadwin and he wasn't sure he wanted to, but she had threatened the guard and stolen his keys, so it was clear she hadn't made any sort of bargain with him.

He hadn't been able to sleep at all with the hard bench and the rats, and lord alone knew how many fleas in that straw, but he doubted she had either. Now it was dark, really dark. The only light these people had came from the moon and that was hidden behind a cloud.

"What now?" Rachel asked.

"You rescued me, so it's up to you."

"Well, the Earl is locked in his bedroom and probably has a concussion, the guard is locked in the dungeon, so it rather depends on how soon they are found, doesn't it? Have you got any money left? We need to get back to London."

"I have but we won't find a carriage at this time of night. Everyone's asleep and when they wake up, they'll probably be looking for us."

"I took the keys to the Earl's bedroom," she

said.

"Really? So, if he has a spare set, he won't have any trouble getting them in the keyhole, will he?"

"Oh. I never thought of that."

They'd walked about a mile away from the castle, both being too weary to run, and now they came to the main village and what looked like a convent. Attached to the building was a small church and Peter clutched her hand and pulled her towards it.

"That's just what we need," Peter said.

"What, your idea of getting us out of this mess is to pray?"

He clucked his tongue at her, shook his head and carried on dragging her toward the little stone building. The stone was almost new, not blackened and weather beaten like it would be when they got home. If they got home.

"A church," he said. "Sanctuary; they won't come after us there."

"It'll be locked at this time of night," Rachel remarked.

He grinned condescendingly and shook his head again.

"This is a house of God," he said. "People did not vandalise churches in this era. They really believed that God was here, inside, and would strike them dead. Churches were never locked."

He was right. He pushed the door open and she followed him inside. That smell of animal fat was back again, only this time it was stale, like a cooker that hadn't been cleaned recently.

"What is that stink, Pete?" Rachel asked.

"Tallow," he replied. "Candles made from animal fat."

"My God! How could they stand the stench?"

"No choice, love. What's more, it's all we've got to use."

One candle burned in a candle holder behind the altar and the smell grew stronger as they moved towards it. There were no pews for worshippers to sit on. It was just one big, hollow space with many statues around the edges. The floor was plain stone, no rushes or mats here, and they could see nothing else to use as mattresses, but they were too tired to care.

"We must sleep," Peter said. "No matter how hard the floor. What do you say?"

She nodded and they settled down behind the altar, wrapped in their cloaks and each other's arms in the vague hope of getting a few hours sleep.

***

They would never have believed they could sleep on a hard, stone floor, but the tensions of the days had left them both exhausted. They might have slept longer, were it not for the interruption of the loud voice of a nun.

She sounded horrified as she hovered over the sleeping couple, her fat arms on her fat hips and disapproval painted all over her face.

"What on earth is going on here?" she demanded.

They came to gradually, opening their eyes to wonder where they were before they remembered the day before and the trouble they had got themselves into.

Peter scrambled stiffly to his feet, reached out a hand to pull Rachel to hers. Neither had ever felt their limbs so inflexible, not even after an all night party and sleeping rough on someone's floor after getting drunk. And Lord, how painful it was to move.

"Nothing, Sister," Peter said. "We had nowhere else to go."

"Debauchery in God's house!" she cried.

"We're married," Rachel said, holding up the finger that wore the wedding ring and wiggling it.

"I've only your word for that," said the nun.

"We were just leaving," said Peter.

"What a way to live," Rachel muttered. "I'd rather kill myself."

She'd meant her tone to be low, so that no one

would hear her, but she forgot the echoing nature of the church. Her voice bounced around the empty building, causing the outraged nun to close her eyes and cross herself.

"Suicide is a mortal sin," she declared. "'Tis not something about which to jest."

Rachel was angry. She'd had enough, one way or the other, and she hadn't forgotten that she hadn't wanted to come on this trip in the first place. She turned one of her fiercest glares on the sister.

"How would my taking my own life be any more of a sin than you burying yourself alive in this place?" She demanded.

"I am a bride of Christ," the nun said. "I have devoted my life to God."

"So I can't top myself, but it's ok for you to cut yourself off from the world in favour of your imaginary friend?"

The nun's mouth dropped open, her eyes opened wide, she crossed herself again, but she had no chance to speak before Peter grabbed Rachel's hand and ran out of the church, dragging her behind him.

"Do you want to get us charged with heresy, as well as witchcraft?" he said.

"Sorry," Rachel answered. "I couldn't help myself."

They had run far enough away from the

church to slow down and walk a little way. The village was waking up, the tradesmen opening up their premises and getting ready to start the day.

"I'm so thirsty," Rachel said. "I could really murder a cup of tea or coffee. I don't suppose there's any chance of getting one here, is there?"

"Not likely. No one had heard of either and the water's not safe. Come on, we might find a spring if we're lucky.

"Now can we rent a carriage to take us back to London?" Rachel said.

"I'm afraid to chance it," Peter replied. "This is only a little place. Probably the only carriage hire will already have been warned about us."

"Then how are we going to get back to London?" she said.

"I think we might have to walk."

"Walk?" Rachel was horrified. "It's miles!"

"Well, I don't know how to ride a horse and neither do you. We can't hire a carriage without arousing suspicion and we can't buy one either."

"Why not? We've got enough money from the necklace, haven't we?"

"Possibly, but I know even less about driving a horse than I do about riding one."

***

The weather warmed as the day wore on, and the couple plodded rather than walked the many miles towards London. They attracted many curious stares, dressed up like nobility with no transport and by the time they reached Shoreditch, they were sweaty, dirty and dishevelled.

Rachel was on the verge of tears the whole way, though she tried her best to be the twenty first century liberated woman she was.

They stopped at a cookshop and managed to buy a pie for their lunch, although they avoided asking exactly what the pie contained. It tasted like lamb, but they'd rather not know.

The strangest thing for Rachel was that what were busy suburbs of London in their time were pretty little villages here. London had not yet stretched out as far as this and they had just got into Shoreditch when a horse and cart drew up beside them.

"You look like you could do with a lift," the driver said.

The man looked rough, very rough. He hadn't shaved in days, but the growth on his chin and face was not yet a beard. He wore a thin, dirty shirt and breeches down to his knees, but the idea of riding for some of the way was too tempting to resist.

"You are very kind, Sir," said Peter.

"Where are you going?" asked the driver.

"High Holborn," Rachel blurted out, then clamped a hand over her own mouth.

"Closer to London, please," Peter said quickly.

But the driver was smiling, a knowing smile that sent a chill down Rachel's spine.

"You're the lady who tried to kill Lord Chadwin," he said. "You're the couple who were digging up earth from a grave."

"How do you know?"

"Word travels fast," he said. "Jump in. I'll get you to High Holborn."

They exchanged glances as they climbed up beside the driver. There was only just enough room for all three of them on the driver's bench, but after their night on the church floor, they were prepared to put up with anything.

Their main concern was, how did the driver know High Holborn? Perhaps he was just repeating what Rachel had inadvertently said, but Peter didn't think so. He sounded more like them than the other people they'd so far met, and although he wasn't very clean, he lacked the inground dirt of the locals.

"Tom's the name," he said. "I'll say no more. I've got a good idea where you two came from, and it's not Whitehall Palace, is it?"

"I don't know what you mean," said Peter.

"Oh, I think you do. Came through the antique shop, didn't you?"

Startled into silence, Rachel's eyes met Peter's and they swallowed. The road was so bumpy, they tasted again the meat pie they had eaten and for a few minutes they rocked about, holding on to each other and waiting for the driver to tell them more. But nothing more was forthcoming.

"You know about the antique shop?" said Rachel.

"Yep. That's how I got here, three years ago."

"You can't have," Rachel argued. "My uncle died sixty years ago and nobody has been inside the shop since."

"Is that so?" said Tom. "I'm really sorry to hear about your uncle, but your sixty years is my three. It was 1940 when I came through the shop, when your uncle helped me come here. He gave me a coin and these clothes, some extra money and told me to go out the front."

"A coin?" Peter said. "An Edward V gold coin?"

"That's right. He had a few of them and he told me to keep it safe, cos I might need it if I ever wanted to come back."

"A few of them?"

"That's right. I'll come clean. I was a deserter from the war. I couldn't stand it any more and I thought, to hell with it and I ran away. I was a coward, I suppose, but I didn't see it that way. Hitler invaded the Channel Islands and I wasn't sticking around for that. It was pretty obvious who was going to win."

Peter and Rachel exchanged a glance, Peter shook his head.

"You came here intentionally?"

"Well, I suppose so, but I didn't know it at the time." Tom paused for a moment, as though trying to find the easiest way to explain. "See, I came home on leave and my wife was carrying on with my brother. He'd escaped being called up because he had something wrong with his foot, but there was apparently nothing wrong with his other bits."

Rachel giggled, but Peter didn't see the joke. He was still busy trying to get his brain around the driver's tale.

"How did you meet Rachel's uncle?"

"He had a lucrative little business going," Tom said. "Helping deserters and other criminals escape justice. He helped a couple of murderers escape the noose, that I do know."

"And they all came here?" Rachel said. "Who else will we find? Lord Lucan?"

"Who?" said Tom.

"Never mind," Peter said. "You say he had several gold coins? We only found one in the shop."

"He must have used all the others," Tom said. "Probably not the best age to stay in, considering who else he sent here. When he said he could get me out of trouble and away from everything, the last thing I expected was to slip back a few centuries. He did tell me, but I didn't believe him. Anyway, I set myself up with a little delivery business and I buy and sell things. It's quiet and easy enough to hide if anyone starts another bloody war."

"He could have changed history," Rachel remarked.

"Yeah, and we wouldn't even know it," said Peter.

"You say the old boy's dead," said Tom. "So what happened? Who won? The poxy Nazis I suppose."

"No," said Peter. "The Japanese bombed Pearl Harbour in 1941, forcing the Americans into the war. We won; Adolf topped himself."

"Good. I'm still glad I went, though. They shoot deserters in wartime."

"Here's a thought," said Rachel. "If you came back with us, would you be in your time or ours?"

Tom shrugged, snorted a laugh, then drew the horse to a stop. They had arrived, outside the row of barns where the antique shop was. It was very quiet, just a few stragglers traipsing along the dirt track, one leading a donkey, another a cow.

"Thank you, Tom," Peter said. "I don't know what we'd have done without your help."

"No problem. I owe it to your uncle and I'm glad Adolf lost."

They watched him drive away, still bemused by the information he had imparted.

"It'd be nice to stay and tell him everything else that's happened," said Rachel.

"Yeah, right. I don't know about you, girl, but I just want to get into a nice hot shower, with some nice twenty first century soap and shampoo. I think, before we try that again, we ought to study the era a bit."

"Again?" Rachel was shaking her head. "Never in a million years are you getting me to do that again."

Peter made no reply as he unlocked the door. *That's what she said last time.*

***

It was raining outside. Heat waves in England nearly always ended in wild thunder storms and the pair hadn't thought about that when they came here in their flimsy summer clothes. But then, they hadn't intended to stay overnight, if that's what they had done. It seemed like weeks since they last saw these streets.

The traffic outside was thick and noisy; was it Monday still, or Tuesday? Or maybe later. Either way, they didn't want to waste time getting soaked outside the shop, and they ran to the entrance to the underground car park. Rachel was thankful for the hefty limit on her credit card, as leaving her car overnight was not cheap.

There always seemed to be a lot more traffic about in the rain, and it all seemed to be driven by impatient drivers with a serious infatuation for their horns. The splashing and the noise might have been something they complained about before this, but now it all looked like the most beautiful sight and sound in the world.

Rachel shivered as the wet seeped into her flesh. There was so much she wanted to say to Peter, but she couldn't find the words. The cold wet was soaking into her tiny summer clothing and she couldn't stop shivering, couldn't keep her teeth from chattering. But even without all that, it seemed a little odd to be discussing their adventures in the fifteenth century here, with all the noisy, wet and absolutely beautiful London traffic.

"Make coffee," Rachel said as she stepped into her shower room at the flat. "Or tea. I'll go first, since it's my flat and my shower."

Then she pulled off her wet clothes and

disappeared beneath the steaming hot water. She stayed under there for fifteen minutes or so, wallowing in the sweet smelling shampoo and the luxurious soap suds.

"Come on, Rache," Peter called out. "Your coffee's getting cold and so am I. I'm freezing too."

Serves you right, she thought, but she rubbed her hair with the towel and pushed her arms into the soft, towelling robe she kept hanging behind the door.

"I hope you're not sitting on my sofa in your wet jeans," she called out as she opened the door.

He wasn't; he was sitting cross legged on the wooden floor, sipping his drink and wearing nothing but his damp boxer shorts. She laughed.

"All yours," she said.

He leapt to his feet and almost ran passed her, slamming the bathroom door and letting it bounce back, so that it wasn't quite shut. Rachel shrugged, then reached for her coffee. It was nothing she hadn't seen before.

CHAPTER EIGHT
The House in Notting Hill

After a day of discussing their journey into the past and a night's sleep on her soft and expensive mattress, Rachel drove Peter back to the flat he shared with some acquaintances so he could pack up his clothes. It didn't seem likely that he was ever going back there, as their recent experiences were not something he could share with anyone else.

"Don't you need to give notice?" she asked him as they drove away.

"I doubt they'll even miss me," he answered. "I've paid up till the end of the month. What about you? Are you going to give up the flat?"

"I'll have to see what sort of state the house is in first and get it valued. I don't feel like sitting on a few million. Either way, I'll get something with room for you."

"If you stay there for a few years, you won't have to pay capital gains tax when you do sell. That'd be worth it, wouldn't it? Why line the government's pockets?"

She would certainly give it some thought. It hadn't occurred to her before, but she wasn't sure how inheritance tax worked so she'd have to see an accountant. Anyway, it could wait for now.

She had taken pity on Peter last night and allowed him to sleep with her. The bed was a kingsize and after all, she wasn't exactly his type.

"Where to next?" he asked her as he shoved his suitcase into the boot of her car. "The house or the churchyard?"

"Do you know what?" she replied. "I'd actually forgotten what we went to Essex for in the first place. I suppose we'd better do that first, see if the journal's still there. It'd better be, after the trouble it got us into."

It wasn't far, once they'd overcome the London traffic, and she pulled up outside the little church and climbed out of the car. But she found it difficult to move. She looked about at the new buildings that had sprung up since their last visit, at the cars parked along the side of the road.

"Come on," Peter said. "Let's get it over with. I can't wait to see if it worked."

"Wait. I just want to assure myself that we're not going to get taken away and charged with witchcraft."

He laughed then started toward the corner of the small churchyard. There was the wall, the same wall built from stacked up stones. The little cross that had marked the child's grave had gone, of course, rotted away over the years and now there was no marker, nothing to tell the world that there were any remains beneath this earth.

Rachel stood with her back to Peter, keeping a look out for potential interference from anyone. After their last visit to this place, she was sure there would be some. A middle aged couple carrying flowers passed them by, about twenty yards away. They nodded and smiled then carried on their way, not knowing how Rachel sighed with relief.

"One big change between then and now," she said. "People have learned to mind their own business."

Peter didn't reply. He was too busy digging into the damp earth with his fingers, the heavy rain of yesterday having made things much easier. He was beginning to think someone had got there first, and he wondered why they hadn't heard about a diary written by the young King Edward V. But then, they hadn't checked, had they? Dammit! They had come here without checking on the internet for such a thing. They might have saved themselves a wasted journey.

But then his finger struck something hard and he caught his breath as he dug faster until he found a familiar glass jar. It was too dirty to see through, and covered in green stuff from six hundred years in the earth, but it was there. They had done it. They had found a way to get things from there till now and they could make a fortune.

He held up the jar for Rachel to see, his smile wide. A worm dropped off the jar, making him jump back and hold the jar out at arm's length, then inspected it for more wildlife, but there was none.

"Put it away, Pete," she said. "Come on. We'll go investigate the house next. We should have done that in the first place; we might find something that would have saved us some grief."

Back at her car, Peter opened the boot and from his suitcase, he pulled out a faded shirt. He folded it in two and wrapped the jar in it, covering it in black, wet earth.

"I take it you don't want that shirt," Rachel said.

"I'll soon be able to afford a new one," he replied smugly, then slammed the boot lid down and climbed into the car beside her.

She pulled away and headed toward the London traffic. She didn't tell him she had her doubts about his expectations; let him have his dream for now. She was more interested in finding out what was inside the house.

It had been many years since she had been

there. She came when her mother died and again when she left university. She wanted to see how Aunt Iris was getting on, the last one left in that rambling old house, and to claim what was left of her family. She had no one else, not then, and she knew she was getting on a bit and might need some help.

She wasn't after her money, no matter what anyone thought, but one look at the house would shout that she was worth a bit, even if it was land rich and cash poor.

She had seemed pleased to see her then, but she kept her firmly in the sitting room. Rachel recalled that the house was massive, one of those four storey whitewashed places with black iron railings and a black front door, with steps leading up to it. There were more steps leading down to the basement and she knew that once upon a time all four floors were separately rented as flats. That's where the aunts and uncle, as well as Rachel's father were born, in that basement flat. But as other tenants had moved out, they had gradually rented the rest of the house and eventually, her uncle made enough money to buy the whole building. Now she knew just how he had made it, helping criminals to escape into the past, she felt a little less respect for him.

Notting Hill was once a slum area of London,

a place where poor families squeezed into one room and shared beds with each other and an outside toilet with the other tenants. It was a dirty part of London, a cheap part but now it was the place for the rich to find a convenient niche and the price of property had soared.

Rachel was sure this house would sell for £5million or more and sell quickly at that, but she had to be sure there were no time portals hidden inside. She giggled, thinking about the estate agents details: *Exclusive house in a sought after area. Time portals included.*

She pulled up in the driveway and they got out, then she clicked the remote control on her key to lock the doors. From her shoulder bag she pulled out the house keys and climbed the steps to the front door, Peter close behind her.

He had never been here before and he could not wait to explore the place. It looked enormous from the outside, at least six bedrooms and two or three reception rooms. It would take weeks to have a good look round.

It had been six weeks since the last aunt was rushed into hospital and never came out. The house smelled stale and musty, the stench of an empty dwelling with the underlying smell of old people. Rachel hoped she never got old enough to leave an odour like that in her wake.

She tossed the keys onto a hall table and

hurried passed the old fashioned hallstand that still contained not only her aunts' overcoats, but what looked like a man's coat as well. On the top was a bowler hat, the sort worn by middle aged men and businessmen during the fifties and earlier and there were several men's umbrellas in the rack.

The carpet was worn, but had once been a flower pattern of cream and maroon on a dark blue background. The wallpaper was dark and of a style popular in the forties, the paintwork brown, causing Rachel to think about going straight to the do it yourself shop to get some white paint.

"Why did people use such dark paint?" said Peter.

"Because it doesn't show the dirt, therefore saving a lot of work on the part of the housewives."

"How dirty does white paintwork get?"

"It doesn't. The dark paint's a left over from when they had coal fires and smoky range ovens. That's where the idea of spring cleaning came from as well."

She left him looking around the dismal hallway and went to the sitting room to open the windows. They were those old sash windows and stiff from disuse, but she managed to force them open and she then did the same in the kitchen and the dining room.

"What's in there?" Peter asked.

Rachel's glance followed his to the closed door at the end of the corridor, between the kitchen and the dining room. She took a step towards it, half expecting to see another of those plaques like the one they had found in the shop.

"That was one of the rooms I was never allowed in," she answered. "I think it was Uncle Charlie's study. I know I went to open it once and Aunt Iris threw a fit. I doubt it's been opened since he died."

"Is it locked?"

Rachel shook her head. She only had keys to the outside of the house, the front, side and back doors. If this door was locked, they'd have to break it down.

She turned the knob and it moved, she felt the catch release and opened the door. The blind was down, obscuring any light from outside. It seemed to be a blackout blind, like the ones they used during the war to block any trace of light that might guide the German bombers.

She crossed the room and it up, letting in more sunshine than this room had seen in sixty years. The cobwebs were heavy, the dust was thick and the lingering smell of Uncle Charlie's pipe was trapped inside.

Rachel opened the window. The view was of

the narrow vegetable garden, which had grown no vegetables in centuries, and now she turned back to look at the heavy, Victorian desk, one of those with a scroll top. It was open and inside were some book slots containing what looked like hard backed diaries, the sort one could buy at any stationers.

The only other furniture were bookcases, mostly containing history books, obviously so that Uncle Charlie knew what he was doing on his trips into the past.

"We should have come here first," she said. "If we'd had the sense to read all this stuff, we might have stayed out of trouble."

"Yes, but we're still here. And it was my fault; I thought I knew what I was doing. I had no idea people were so inquisitive."

"Nosy, you mean."

"If you like."

He pulled one of the diaries from the desk and opened it up. It was dated 1950, but inside there was another date, 1554. He began to read, but then a photograph fell from the pages and he took it to the window to study it further.

It was black and white and he recognised the woman in the picture immediately, and the man with his lantern jaw confirmed it.

"What have you got there?" Rachel asked.

He held it out to her.

"It seems your uncle was clever enough to take a camera on his travels. If I'm not very much mistaken, that is a picture of Queen Mary I of England and her bridegroom, Prince Philip of Spain."

She laughed, an involuntary snigger that told him she suspected him of joking. His grave expression silenced her and she pulled the photograph from his hand and stared at it.

If there was one period of history that had interested her, it was the reign of Bloody Mary and she had seen portraits of the woman in this photograph enough times to agree with Peter.

"A photograph of Bloody Mary," she said. "An actual sodding photograph of Bloody Mary."

He stood behind her and stared at the picture over her shoulder. It was the most fascinating thing either of them had ever laid eyes on.

"It'll take weeks, or even months, to get through this lot and that's without the stuff your aunts left behind. You can't sell this place, not until we've explored."

"No, I can't. I'll give up the flat and we'll move in here, just for the time being. I wonder how many more photographs he has. I've never seen a picture of Elizabeth I that actually looked like anyone."

"I think a lot of the artists painted to please

the subject. That's why Oliver Cromwell ordered that his portrait was real, warts and all."

"Is that where the saying comes from?"

She dragged her eyes away from the photograph when she felt his fingers tighten on her arm.

"Do you realise what this means?" he said.

"Yes. We have photographs of historical people, taken before anyone invented the camera. Not that they are worth anything, in monetary value. After all, who's going to believe they're genuine?"

"That's not what I meant. If your uncle could take a camera back to the past and take photographs, it means that, although we can't bring anything from there to here, we can do it the other way round."

"And what good does that do us?"

His mouth twisted thoughtfully, then he sighed and shrugged.

"You're right. Apart from the camera, there's not a lot that'd work, is there?"

"We could take some scissors, I suppose, some fine needles and thread, but that's about all." She caught sight of a photograph in a silver frame on the window sill. She hadn't noticed it before. "I wonder who this is?" she said.

It was a black and white photograph of a woman in Elizabethan costume, her hair covered in the usual sort of headdress that they wore then. It was pretty hair, dark, either brunette or auburn and her eyes were wide. She was smiling, a happy smile, not the wistful sort of smile one sometimes saw in portraits of the time. Rachel supposed that was because they had to pose for so long, their mouths would cramp up.

Behind the glass, faded writing could be seen on the photograph itself. Rachel picked it up and brought it closer to her eyes.

To Charles, with my undying love, Isabel.

"Charles? Your uncle?" said Peter.

"Yes. Charlie Jarrod."

"You don't think he found love somewhere in the past, do you?"

"Possibly. Or perhaps he had a lady friend here and now and persuaded her to dress up in one of the costumes from the shop." She put the photograph back in its place. "I never heard of such a person, but then it seems I didn't know the half of what was going on."

She turned back to the desk to look through the other diaries, but Peter wanted to study the photograph some more. The woman was rather lovely, but it was the background in which he was interested, horses and carriages, peasants in medieval dress leading donkeys, goats and cows.

***

They chose bedrooms in the house and Rachel went back to her flat to pack her clothes. She gave notice to her landlord and settled into the enormous room she had chosen.

The wardrobes were those old, mahogany monstrosities from the pre-war era and there was a hideous dresser to match. They would be going on Ebay, as soon as she could afford to replace them.

Peter had scoured the internet for any sign of a journal written by the young King Edward V and found nothing. Now all he had to do was get the scroll authenticated and come up with a plausible tale to explain how he found it.

"Well, you can't say it was buried in a glass jar," Rachel told him.

"No. I doubt they used glass for jars, more like stone or clay. I think the Dead Sea Scrolls were discovered in a clay jar; that had kept them safe for nearly two thousand years." He put a new phrase into the search engine. "I might have to buy a stone jar, bury it for a week or so in your garden here, then pretend that's where we found it."

"It might work."

She stripped the beds and changed the sheets

for her own, dumped the blankets and replaced them with quilts from her own bed. Luckily, she had a spare in the airing cupboard at the flat, so there was one for Peter as well.

They ordered another takeaway then settled down to inspect the contents of the study and begin reading the diaries. They were fascinating, but Rachel had a hard time sleeping that night, after reading about Uncle Charlie's adventures in another time, how he watched the heretics being burned alive at Smithfield, how he had watched public hangings, but drew the line at the public spectacle of hanging, drawing and quartering.

The following day, after driving to the supermarket to collect supplies, they settled down again to read more.

"This stuff is sickening," Rachel said. "How can a civilised man from the twentieth century watch this stuff?"

Peter shrugged.

"Who knows? Perhaps it was the fascination of it. A public execution of any sort would outrage most people now, but then it was a day's outing for the family."

Rachel made no reply. She had found a diary dated 1480, a year when the wars of the roses were still going on, and now she was reading about a soldier who had deserted from World

War II.

He had deserted, and who could blame him? Wrote Charlie. *He came home, expecting his wife to welcome him, only to find his brother had moved in and it was obvious what they'd been up to.*

For a year he'd been killing people; he thought he could manage two more and at least this time he had a reason. The police knew it was him and they were looking for him.

He signed his house over to me then I sent him back. He didn't know about history, he was just desperate to escape the noose. I thought it ironic that he had run away from one war and I was sending him to another one. I don't know how he got on, don't know if the war affected him. Perhaps I shouldn't have done it, but I rented the house out so made a nice little income from it. I left it to the girls in my Will.

There was a photograph of the man, in his army uniform, and there was no mistaking the driver who had given them a lift on his cart.

She passed the diary to Peter.

"I can't believe my uncle would do this," she said. "The man deserved to hang."

"You believe in the death penalty?"

"If it's justified, yes."

"You surprise me."

"Why? I don't believe in the barbaric executions they had in the past, but that's different. Of course, for some of them, death is too good."

"Who are the girls, do you think?"

"My aunts, I imagine. Perhaps they sold the house; they must have had some income to keep this place going."

***

Peter found an expert on medieval documents and after much agitation, was persuaded to leave the scroll with him. His name was Professor Carlton and Peter found him in the medieval history department at Oxford University. Those credentials should be trustworthy enough, but after everything they had suffered to bring it here, he was reluctant to part with the precious document.

"I'll give you a receipt," said Professor Carlton. "This is a major find."

"I know. You can understand I am anxious to find out if it's genuine."

He wasn't a good liar and even this one little white one had caused his innards to churn. Lord alone knew how he was going to manage when the television cameras were pointed at him and journalists were wanting to know all the details of his miraculous find.

"You found it in your garden, you say?" said

the Professor.

"Yes. Well, my friend's garden She inherited the house from her aunt and the garden is enormous. Who knows what else is there? Possibly old Roman ruins."

"And you managed to decipher enough to decide this was a journal written by one of the lost princes?"

"I have a lot of experience of medieval documents," he replied. "But I needed someone else to authenticate it. I hope I'm doing the right thing."

"Indeed you are, young man. If it's genuine, this find will be as sensational as the Dead Sea Scrolls."

Peter swallowed, picked up his receipt and tried to keep himself from fleeing. He was never going to manage this. He stood up, ready to force himself to walk slowly away.

"By the way," said the Professor, stopping him. "The jar you found this in. Do you have it?"

Peter had anticipated this question and decided on a plausible answer.

"Unfortunately not. The fact is, I was digging in the corner when I found it. The shovel shattered it, but I think it was some sort of clay."

"Pity. Never mind. I will call you as soon as I have a definitive answer for you. And Dr Attwood..."

"Yes?"

"Thank you so much for bringing this to me. I am in your debt."

Outside in the quad, Peter breathed a heavy sigh of relief. Thank goodness the Professor had asked no further questions, or Peter might have forgotten his previous answers. As it was, he had already imagined a tale of a dead cat found on the road to excuse his digging. He hadn't had to use it, but he might need to save it for later.

They had moved into the house, painted over that dreary brown paintwork with a clean, glossy white which had cheered the place up no end. Peter had the second floor at the top of the house, Rachel used the rooms on the first floor for her bedroom and her workroom. They had so far not decided about the basement flat. When Peter sold the journal, they were planning on totally refurbishing it and renting it out.

The ground floor they both used; that's where the kitchen was and access to the garden. Peter had told no lie; it was enormous and one of the few along the street that had not been sold off for building.

So they settled in. Peter was still working at the museum, but hoping to be able to give that up soon and concentrate on writing. Rachel's own label was doing reasonably well, too. It wasn't Versace and probably never would be, but it was gaining some respect.

In between work, they were still ploughing through the mounds of diaries and photographs Uncle Charlie had left behind.

Peter returned from his visit to the Oxford professor to find Rachel in the kitchen, eating an egg salad for her lunch. She'd left him some, already on a plate covered in cling film.

"There's tea in the pot," she said. "If you want coffee, you'll have to make it. How did it go?"

"Ok," he said. "Better than I expected, really. He's going to get back to me. He reckons it could be a big as the Dead Sea Scrolls and if it is, I just hope I can keep up the pretence."

"Well, you can hardly tell him the truth, can you?" she said. "Anyway, I had five new orders for the winter collection today, so we might be able to update this wretched kitchen soon."

He looked around at the old fashioned kitchen units. They were wooden, painted a bilious pale green which was badly chipped round the edges. He couldn't deny that it desperately needed doing, but he had other things on his mind.

"What are you doing for Christmas?" he asked.

"That's months away."

"Yes, but even so. Time'll go quick enough."

"Well, I don't bother too much with

Christmas," she said as she sipped her tea. "Why? You do what you want. We might be sharing the house, but we don't have to live in each other's pockets."

"I just thought it would be really great fun to see a medieval Christmas. They went on for the full twelve days, you know."

She put down her mug and glared at him, her eyes wide and accusing and she shook her head.

"No way," she said after a moment. "I am never going back in time, never again. If you want to risk it, you can go on your own."

Peter removed the cling film from his plate of salad and put it on the table, then he sat down and began to eat. *We shall see*, he thought.

Thank you for reading Ye Olde Antique Shoppe: The Edward V Coin. I hope you have enjoyed it and if you have, please leave a review.

Books Two and Three in the series, the Anne Boleyn Necklace and The Ripper Rings are now available. If you wish to have notice of it and all future releases, please subscribe to my mailing list on my website at www.margaret-brazear.com. You can also claim some free e-books.

Please consider my other books:

The Holy Poison Series:

The Judas Pledge
The Flawed Mistress
The Viscount's Birthright
Betrayal
The Heretics
Consequences

The Pestilence Series:

The Second Wife

The Scent of Roses
Once Loved (winner of the 2017 e-festival of words best historical)

The Elizabethans Series:

The Earl's Jealousy
The Viscount's Divorce
Lord John's Folly

The Hartleighs of Somersham:

A Match of Honour – Winner of 2018 efestival of words Best Historical Romance
Lady Penelope's Frenchman

Standalone novels:

The Minstrel's Lady (winner of the 2017 e festival of words Best Romance)
The Gorston Widow
The Crusader's Widow
The Wronged Wife
To Catch a Demon
The Cavalier's Pact
The Adulteress
Conquest
Shed No Tears

A Man in Mourning
The Outcast
The Romany Princess

The Loves of the Lionheart – History's Forgotten Princesses
For the Love of Anne – Anne Boleyn's First Love

Fantasy – The Surrogate Bride
Thriller/mystery – Old Fashioned Values

Printed in Great Britain
by Amazon